A SONGBIRD IN FLIGHT

Michael Rodney Moore

D1195636

Copyright © 2022 Michael Rodney Moore

All rights reserved

The characters and events portrayed in this book are fictitious. Any similarity to real persons, living or dead, is coincidental and not intended by the author.

No part of this book may be reproduced, or stored in a retrieval system, or transmitted in any form or by any means, electronic, mechanical, photocopying, recording, or otherwise, without express written permission of the publisher.

This book is dedicated to my sweet Debbie Rose!

Thank you for reading and making my work better!
I will always love you more!

CONTENTS

CHAPTER 1 • THE CAGE

Veronica Tillman was busy browsing for a present for her son's upcoming birthday when the phone rang at her desk. She glanced at the caller ID and immediately answered the phone.

"Good afternoon, this is Culpepper Wealth Management. How may we help you?" she asked as professionally as she could even though she knew who was on the line.

"Yes, Veronica! Percy Brigston calling. I would like to speak with Roger but first, how are you and that wonderful son of yours doing?" asked the aristocratic British-accented voice on the line.

"We are both doing marvelously. Thank you for asking , Mr. Brigston," she replied to the friendly voice of Culpepper Wealth Management's only client.

"Wonderful! As I recall, young Master Theodore will be having a birthday soon. Please be expecting a gift from me. Now be so kind as to put me through to that braggart that you work for," the cultured voice said with good humor.

Veronica placed Percy Brigston on hold as she announced the call to her boss, Roger Culpepper.

"Mr. Brigston is on the line, Roger," she announced and saw that Roger had picked up the line without even acknowledging her. This had been her life since she was eighteen and just graduated from high school. It was only going to be a summer job.

"Only a summer job," she remembered, and blushed at just what a turn her life took thirteen years ago.

Veronica had been an impressionable young woman who had grown up in a family that consisted of only her mother and herself. They had always struggled to get by. Her mother worked as a waitress and often worked multiple jobs to pay the rent and put food on the table. Veronica had grown up wearing clothes that were purchased at thrift stores and yard sales. It was this lifestyle that drove her to be an honor-roll student so that she could go to college to earn a better living. She hated being poor and vowed to never be poor again. She had managed to get a scholarship to an exclusive private high school where she had excelled academically but was always a social outcast among her wealthy fellow students.

Just before she graduated, she was looking for a summer job that involved anything other than waiting tables or fast food. One of her teachers found out that she was looking for work and introduced her to Roger Culpepper. Apparently Roger was a significant booster to the school, which he had attended as a youth.

That first meeting played over in her mind as she sat back in her chair. She had been so naive. She had been informed that the interview would be over dinner at an exclusive private club. Her mother took her to an upscale clothing store and purchased a tailored business suit for her. Veronica would never forget the first look at herself in the mirror. She looked beautiful and professional.

"You look the part, baby," her mother said as her eyes moistened at the sight of her only child all grown up and important-looking.

"Thank you, Momma!" she had replied as they embraced.

That evening she arrived at the exclusive club at the top of one of Atlanta's tallest buildings. Dinner was to be at six but Veronica arrived five minutes early. The entire experience was both intimidating and exciting.

"Good evening, Miss. How may we serve you?" asked the immaculately-dressed hostess with a Miss America smile.

"I'm here to have dinner with Roger Culpepper," Veronica

replied nervously.

"He called and said that he would be a few minutes late but that I should go ahead and seat you. Please follow me," the hostess said as her stunning smile flashed across her beauty-queen face again.

Veronica was mystified as the woman walked her past the main dining room and then into a private room which had a breathtaking view of the city below. As they reached the table a black man in a tailored tuxedo joined them, pulled a chair from the table, and indicated that Veronica should be seated.

"This is Robert and he will be serving you this evening," the hostess said as she held her hand towards the man. "Please enjoy your meal and we hope that you will come again," she said before she turned and left the room.

"May I bring you a cocktail while you await Mr. Culpepper?" the waiter asked in a deep cultured voice.

Veronica had no idea what was appropriate under the circumstances so she said, "I will wait for Mr. Culpepper to arrive, thank you."

"Very well, Miss," he said with a slight bow as he left the room.

Veronica looked down and saw the array of forks, knives, and spoons along with a linen napkin and wine and water glasses. It was all so overwhelming that she began to wonder just how big of a fool would she make of herself before dinner was over?

Then a waitress entered the room with a pitcher and bottle on a tray. The young woman was very petite with hair pulled back in a French braid. Her uniform fit like a glove and showed great attention to detail on the part of the management of the club.

"I'm Stacy and I will be your assistant waitress this evening. Would you prefer sparkling water?" she asked.

"Please," Veronica said even though she had never had sparkling water before.

Stacy had just finished pouring the bubbly water when Roger entered the room.

"Good evening, Mr. Culpepper. Would you care for sparkling water?" Stacy asked.

"Yes, that would be fine, Stacy," he said to the waitress and then turned to Veronica and looked her over as he smiled. "I'm Roger Culpepper and you must be Veronica Tillman! It is a pleasure to finally meet you," he said as he took her hand and squeezed it while he looked into her eyes.

The head waiter arrived in time to assist Roger in taking his seat.

"Good evening, Mr. Culpepper," the man said in his rich, cultured voice. "This evening our chef has prepared two specials in addition to our normal menu. The first is Lobster Thermidor with a grilled vegetable medley. The chef recommends a Caesar salad for the starter. The second is a blackened grilled snapper which is paired with fingerling potatoes and creamed spinach. The chef also recommends the Caesar for the starter. Would you care for a cocktail to begin?"

"Yes, please bring us each a vodka tonic," he said without hesitation, even though he knew his dinner companion was only eighteen.

Robert left the room and again Veronica felt the older man look her over. Roger was thirty-nine at that time. He was fit and extremely good looking, dressed comfortably in his expensive suit and Italian loafers. He had a thick gold wedding band on his ring finger. His hair was neatly done and his hands were manicured. She was certain this man had never known lean times.

"So, Veronica, I hear that you are looking for a summer intern position," Roger said to begin the conversation.

"Yes, I have been accepted to Georgia State this fall and I would like to make a little money before I start in August," she replied but she felt like a fish out of water.

Robert returned with their drinks which were carried by Stacy who deftly served them and then turned and left.

"Would you like more time before ordering dinner?" the waiter asked in his rich voice.

Roger looked at Veronica who was in a panic as what to do. She had never been anywhere like this before but the older and more confident man took the situation in hand.

"Please allow me to order for you, my dear," Roger offered with a reassuring smile before proceeding. "The lady will have the lobster and I will have snapper. Perhaps you could bring us a bottle of your best Pinot Grigio?"

"Excellent selection as always, Mr. Culpepper," Robert intoned before he left the table.

"May I ask you a personal question, Veronica?" Roger asked as he lifted his cocktail to his lips.

"Certainly," Veronica said with a nod.

"Are you going to school to make money?" he asked as he studied her.

"It would be nice to be able to make a good income," she replied.

"I take it you have never been around money before. I checked on your family and you were raised by your mother with very limited means. I suspect that tonight will be the first time you have tasted lobster. I would also surmise that your outfit is the first set of brand new clothes you have ever had," he said as he took another sip and continued. "The American dream is to get an education and then you will get all the money you will ever need. Unfortunately, it is a fraud," Roger said as he looked intently into her eyes. "Most people will never earn all of the money they would like and their spending will always outstrip what they do have."

Veronica tried to think of something to say.

Before she could say anything, however, he resumed. "You are obviously an extremely intelligent woman and, if I might add, a very lovely one as well. Education is one way to try to get ahead but it is not the surest way of being successful, whether in terms of money or position. What always leads to money and power is whom you know. If you know the right people, money will find its way to you." He paused for a moment as he looked her over again. "I am one of those people who can see to it that money will never be a problem for you again. The question I must find the answer to is are you willing to take care of my needs so that I can give you all the things you have ever wanted and so much more?"

Veronica was stunned at how the conversation had turned. Just what was this man interviewing her for?

Then Robert and Stacy returned with the salads and a bottle of wine. As Robert served the wine, Veronica reached for the vodka tonic and then drank it down to try and calm her nerves. As she set the glass back down, she looked back at Roger who was smiling with delight.

The wait staff once again retreated from the room and left them alone. They both took a couple of bites of the salad, which was fabulous.

Then Roger said, "I will need to get know you much more intimately if you would like me to see to your financial needs."

Veronica blushed as she now knew for sure what this wealthy and powerful man was after. If she gave herself to him, he might make her his mistress. She felt her mind spinning at the thought of becoming a kept woman but on the other hand she would never be poor again.

"Okay," she said quietly as her desire to never be poor again won out.

Roger reached for her hand and she looked down to see his left hand on her own. Her eyes locked on the large gold wedding band and knew for sure what was expected.

Before the night was over she experienced her first gourmet meal as well as her first sex with a married man.

Veronica was snapped back to the present when the door to Roger's office suddenly opened. To her surprise, Roger looked shaken as he walked to her desk but he quickly regained his composure. He looked down at her and smiled.

"Percy needs me to take care of a situation for him up in Charlotte. Call the airport and tell the pilots to have the plane ready in thirty minutes. Obviously I will not be coming over tonight so Teddy can just stay home," he said as he bent and kissed her on the head before rushing back into his office. Her son, Teddy, was always shipped off to a nanny's home to spend the night when Roger planned on "visiting" his mom.

The kiss was not one of affection but was intended to maintain possession. She had been his mistress for thirteen years and with a shudder she knew that was all she would ever be until he had no more use for her.

She called the pilots and alerted them of the sudden travel. Even after all these years, Veronica was not exactly sure what Roger did for Mr. Brigston. She knew that he managed a lot of investments but there were other things that often made no sense, such as tracking shipping containers, moving funds around the world, and, like tonight, going off and meeting with people at a moment's notice.

Roger reappeared from his office. He had changed into casual travel clothes and was carrying a large gym bag and a smaller brief case. She looked at him and noticed that he looked nervous and frankly a little rattled.

"I should be back the day after tomorrow. Call my wife and tell her I have an emergency business trip and I will not be home for a week," he said with a wink, "Then book us a suite so I can get some quality time with you."

Veronica cringed at the thought of what she would have to do for him on his return. He walked over and kissed her passionately before he hurried out the door.

Veronica made the call to Roger's wife, which she hated to do. She was sure that his wife was well aware of what her true position was. There was a time when Veronica had hated her but now she felt a certain kindred spirit for the woman whose husband shared her bed.

"Hello, Terresa. This is Veronica. Roger wanted me to call and tell you that he has been called away to an emergency meeting and will not be home for a week," she said as she tried control her guilt.

"Thank you for calling. I hope you enjoy yourself!" the other woman answered tersely before abruptly ending the call.

Veronica felt as if she had been slapped in the face. Again, she could empathize with the other woman. They both were trapped with Roger Culpepper. Teressa must know that her position in

Atlanta society was at risk if she ever left Roger and Veronica knew for a fact that most of his assets were safely hidden away from his wife as well as his mistress.

Her own position was even more tenuous as her condo was owned by a partnership that Roger discretely controlled. If she left him she would have hardly anything with which to start a new life. Worst of all, Roger would make sure that Teddy was taken from her. To say the least she was like a songbird in a gilded cage with a hungry predator waiting at the door to devour her.

She was closing the office when she noticed that Roger had left the door to his office slightly ajar. She opened the door to see if he had forgotten to turn off the lights. As she looked around the room, she could see that he must have forgotten to turn off his computer.

Veronica did not know it but the door to her cage was about to be ripped off its hinges.

CHAPTER 2 • WHO IS ROGER CULPEPPER?

A shaken Roger Culpepper walked out of his office carrying two bags. The first bag was his briefcase, which contained the typical business items such as a note pad, pens, pencils, and reference material such as the personnel file of one Jeffrey Williams. Tonight there were a few other items that were not so typical but none the less essential for the business at hand. There was a Taurus nine-millimeter semiautomatic pistol, a throwaway cell phone, a tranquilizer, a syringe, and a vial of potassium chloride. In the other bag were a change of clothes and one-hundred-thousand dollars in cash.

He put the two bags on the seat beside him as he got into his Benz. It would take about thirty minutes to drive over to Brown Field to meet his two pilots that were kept on call twenty-four hours a day and three-hundred-sixty-five days per year. They would have his Learjet 36A ready to fly.

Roger had a great life. He had tremendous wealth with a personal net worth of over one-hundred-million dollars. In addition, he had access to Percy Brigston's countless billions of dollars and even more important, his influence and power. There was also one other thing that Brigston gave him access to: the endless opportunity to indulge himself with adolescent girls.

Roger felt both exhilaration and disgust at his lifelong fetish for underage sex partners. Many times, he had sought to curb his appetite but just as he thought he could put it behind him, Percy would introduce him to another irresistible Lolita. It was like being a drug addict.

Roger arrived at the gate that would admit him into the hanger area where his jet was housed. Actually, the jet belonged to Brigston but it was there for his exclusive use.

"Good evening, Mr. Culpepper. I hope you have a great trip," the security guard said as he opened the gate.

"Why, thank you, Larry!" he replied and was pleased at his ability to recall the names of the little people who saw to his every need. It always left a good impression on the peons, which did wonders at keeping them motivated.

It was a short drive to the hanger. He parked in a space by the door to the small office and waiting room area. He carried his two bags to the door, which opened as he approached, and one of the pilots held the door open for him.

"Good evening, Mr. Culpepper. May I take your bags to the plane for you?" the pilot asked.

"I can handle it but thank you, Douglas," he replied cheerfully.

"Very well. Jimmy is just finishing filing our flight plan and we should be wheels up shortly," Douglas said as he escorted Roger to the plane.

Soon Roger was comfortably settled in his favorite seat in the four-passenger-capacity light jet while the pilots completed their checklist and then closed the cockpit door, leaving him to his own thoughts. It was then that he relived the phone conversation that he had with Brigston back at the office.

"We have a bit of problem, Roger," Brigston said with his upper-crust British enunciation.

"What sort of a problem?" he asked calmly but could already sense that it was serious.

"Do you recall that detective that we recently put on the payroll in Charlotte?" Brigston asked casually.

"Yes, I think I do," he replied as he quickly opened his files on The Organization on his computer.

Those files were extensive and documented their human assets around the world as well as the accounting of the money that flowed to and from their human trafficking network. There were the sources of new victims such as recruiters and kidnappers, mules that transported the human cargo to where they would be trained and finally delivered to their customers who ranged from street pimps to the wealthy and powerful who truly ran the world. It also contained the corrupt local officials, bureaucrats, and law enforcement officers who glossed over the inevitable screw-ups that were bound to happen in such an enormous enterprise.

"His name is Jeffrey Williams, a detective that works in Vice. He has a gambling problem and a girlfriend in addition to his wife," Roger said as he studied the file further. "He just joined us about ninety days ago."

"That would be the one. He is making a bit of trouble, old man. He has been collecting names of people involved in our operation in Charlotte and is making noise that if he does not get more money he will go to the feds," Brigston said as if he were talking about what he had for lunch.

"How would you like this handled? We could give him a demonstration of our displeasure," Roger said and hoped that this could be limited to a few hours of torture by one of their more experienced trainers. Roger shuddered at the thought of how much pain the trainers could inflict and not leave a mark. Some of their subjects became so broken that they never recovered and would commit suicide.

"I think in this case we must make a strong demonstration that our reach is long and our retribution is final. He will need to be terminated," Brigston intoned Jeffrey William's death sentence.

"Very well, shall it be murder, suicide, or natural causes?" Roger asked as if he wanted to know what the other man wanted to drink.

"I think a natural cause would suffice," Brigston said before adding, "You will personally take care of this so that there are no slip-ups. You will then make it known to our other Charlotte operatives what happens to those that make trouble."

"Of course, Percy. I will be there tonight to get the job done." Roger replied calmly to mask the terror he felt inside as he took on the role of executioner.

"Good show, old man! Plan on coming down to the island next month. I am in process of adding a few fresh faces. One is a lovely ebony from South Africa that I think you will enjoy," Brigston said with a lustful leer in his voice.

"I will look forward to that," Roger said as his heart beat faster.

With the call over he had sat back in his leather chair and closed his eyes to try and calm his nerves. It had been a while since he had committed murder personally. Normally he would just arrange for it to happen. There was also added tension in this case since he had been ordered to make it look like a natural death. To do that he would need to be up close and personal with the victim.

Roger rushed to gather the things that would be needed. He decided the best approach would be to lure Williams to a remote location where he would allow him to see a large bag of money. He would then find a way to use a tranquilizer that would incapacitate the man. Nothing drastic, just something that kept him awake but unable to resist. Followed by a quick jab with a potassium chloride-filled syringe. Then he would simply wait for the heart attack to take care of the problem.

Roger was brought back to the present as he heard the chime indicating that they were about to take off. He felt the acceleration press him back into his leather seat as the jet raced down the runway. He pulled out his cell phone and turned it off. He knew that he did not want anyone to track his movements when he arrived in Charlotte. This was not his first cleanup assignment. He needed to move quietly and leave no trace of his activities once he exited the plane. He had arranged for a car to be delivered to the small airfield where they would land. He had a throwaway phone for calling his target. The gun that he carried could not be traced to him and he had carefully loaded and handled the gun with gloves on to avoid fingerprints. Besides, the gun was only for persuasion or if the wheels came off the plan.

Then he would need to take care of the other issue and that was to make sure that the other operatives knew what had happened to the unfortunate Detective Williams. He would use this as an opportunity to get another law enforcement asset to push the investigation into the closed files and stamped "Death Due to Natural Cause."

He smiled as he at last felt comfortable with his plan. He closed his eyes and started to relax when it hit him like a train! In his rush to leave he had left his computer open to "The Organization" files and he had failed to close the vault that contained his emergency supply of cash, weapons, and worst of all, his "Insurance Policy."

"Did I lock my office door?" he asked himself.

Roger tried to focus his thoughts on what he had done while rushing out tonight but he remained unsure of locking his office door. It would be a disaster if he had not and Veronica looked inside his office and saw the computer still on.

"Maybe Veronica would just close the computer down without looking at it?" he thought but knew that was unlikely.

Besides, there was no way that she would fail to notice the contents of the vault. If she noticed the thumb drive and looked at what it contained, she would be a dead woman walking. If Percy found out he even had that recording on the thumb drive he would be dead as well.

Roger considered telling the pilots to turn around. However, he knew that this would lead to questions in Brigston's mind as to just what his most trusted servant was doing. No, there was only one way to deal with this. First, he would finish the Charlotte assignment as quickly as possible before rushing back to Atlanta to confirm—or assuage--his fears. If confirmed, however, he would have to kill Veronica.

CHAPTER 3 • SECRETS REVEALED

V eronica stepped into Roger's office and it occurred to her that she had never been in it when he was not present in all of the thirteen years that she had been his employee and mistress. It felt strange as she looked around the room and walked toward his desk. Her first thought was to turn off his computer, lock the door, and leave. Before she made it to the computer, however, she saw something that she had never noticed before.

Roger's impressive office was paneled in exotic wood with massive book shelves that held various books and mementos of his life. Tonight, she noticed one of the panels was actually a door that had been left ajar. She opened it and looked into a room. There was a vault door at the far end of the room, which was propped open. Before she reached the vault she realized that the room had cabinets and on the wall were several handguns. She opened the door to the vault and she inhaled sharply. There were stacks of cash organized by country of origin and denomination. She readily recognized euros, pounds, Canadian dollars, and Mexican pesos in addition to ones that she couldn't identify. By far the largest amount of currency was United States dollars.

Then she saw that there were also gold bars stacked on a reinforced shelf. She noticed that there were drawers below the gold. Her hand shook as she opened the first drawer and was stunned to see boxes filled with what appeared to be large diamonds. Each box appeared to hold more than a hundred of the glittering gems. She closed that drawer and opened the one below it and saw a series of page-size envelopes. She noticed that they had various country names on them and picked up the one that was labeled "United Kingdom." In the envelope she found a passport with Roger's picture on the inside but it was not in his name. Quickly looking at the other documents she determined that they would provide Roger with a false British identity as well. There were also several credit cards belonging to the Roger alias. She put that envelope back and counted at least a dozen false identities available and ready to be used.

"Roger, what are you into?" she asked herself as she put the documents back.

She opened the final drawer and the only item there was a single thumb drive. She picked it up and decided she wanted to see what was on it that it would need to be kept in a vault. She stepped back out of the vault and returned to Roger's desk. She was just getting ready to put the thumb drive into his computer when she saw the file that was left open. It was labeled "Organization Human Assets." She looked at the subdirectory titles and noticed they were labeled "Recruiters," "Trainers," "Transporters," and "Fixers." The open file was about a Charlotte Police Department Detective Jeffrey Williams. She noticed that there was a status designation and the word "Terminated" with the next day's date.

Veronica looked at the directory again and saw that there was another folder and this was labeled "Inventory." She opened that file and felt her skin crawl as hundreds of files appeared. She clicked on the first file and started to cry as she saw a photo of a terrified teenage girl. There was a fact sheet of where she came from, her age, and her status, which was currently "in training," as well as her likely monetary value on delivery.

"Oh my God," she moaned as it became clear that each of these files represented a person who was in the process of being sold into prostitution.

Veronica felt on the verge of vomiting. Her eyes landed on the thumb drive from the vault. Part of her wanted to just leave but she needed to know what was on that drive that it had to be kept in the vault with all the other items of immense value. Her hand was shaking so badly that she had trouble putting the drive into the slot on the computer. What she saw next would never leave her mind again as she saw Percy Brigston having sex with an underage girl.

Veronica burst into tears as she stopped the disgusting recording. She tried to get herself under control as she was overwhelmed with revulsion and anger. She realized that she had been an unwitting participant in this abhorrent criminal enterprise that destroyed the innocent for lust and fortunes. Never in her life could she imagine the depravity of what she had just seen.

Veronica realized that Roger would remember that he had been careless very soon. When he did, he would be coming for her. She thought about what she had seen in the hidden room and the vault. She was certain that Roger was more than capable of killing her. She needed to run, and quickly, as he might come back at any moment.

Veronica made some quick decisions. She got another thumb drive from the supply cabinet and began to copy the Organization files from Roger's computer. Then she walked back to the vault and started to stuff as many stacks of one-hundred-dollar bills as she could into a gym bag and then she added several boxes of diamonds. Next she went and got her purse and filled it as well.

She looked at the clock and was shocked that an hour had passed. She picked up her phone and called Teddy's nanny.

"Hi Marsha," she said as the nanny picked up the phone, "There has been a change of plans. Teddy will be coming home tonight. I will be there as quickly as I can."

Veronica put the thumb drives into her purse and turned the computer off, shut the panel door, and closed Roger's office door before she turned off all of the lights and left the office for the last time.

She got into her BMW SUV and realized that the life she had lived for the last thirteen years was now over. Soon she would be just another single mom with no education who would be back to waiting tables and buying clothes for herself and her son at yard sales and thrift stores.

"So much for my dreams," she said but then saw in her mind the picture of that poor abused girl and knew that girl and countless others like her had been the source of all of the wealth that had provided Veronica the extravagant lifestyle that she had lived and that was now gone forever. "Thank God!" she said out loud.

She started to drive to the nanny's house when she looked down and saw that she had about a half a tank of gas.

"Better top off and use the credit card because that will be turned off soon enough," she said to herself and was pleased that she was starting to think ahead.

After getting the gas she went on to pick up Teddy. He was happy to see her as he had expected to spend the night away from his mother. Veronica wondered if even her young son understood that he always went away when "Uncle Roger" came over. Veronica cringed and hoped that her son was not already that worldly.

"Sweety, we need to go away for a little while. We are going home but we need to just gather a few clothes and a couple of your favorite toys," she said in what hopefully sounded like she was being cheerful.

"Mom! I'm not a baby and I don't have toys anymore," he replied but then asked hopefully, "Can I bring my tablet, please?" he asked desperately.

"Fine, but remember we need to travel light." She said as she began to watch who might be following her as paranoia kicked in.

When they arrived at the condominium, she decided she would have to risk leaving the heavy gym bag in the car while they got their things together. She wondered what the value of that bag truly was.

Once in their condo, she quickly tried to gather practical clothes to put into her roller bag. She added other essentials that any woman would need for several days. It was only then that she realized that she had no idea where she was running to or what she could do to keep from being killed by Roger. Then it occurred to her that Teddy's life was also on the line. She sat on the bed and fought to keep from being overwhelmed by tears. She had to focus!

"Think, Veronica," she told herself as she tried to concentrate and then the file of Detective Jeffrey Williams popped into her mind, "Yes, I need to get to him before Roger does!"

"I'm ready, Mom," Teddy said as he stood in the door of her bedroom.

"I'll be right there, baby," she replied as she quickly opened the safe in the closet and cleaned out her jewelry and small stash of cash.

She picked up her purse and was checking the contents when she saw her cell phone. She decided that she should call Jeffrey Williams right away. When she reached for the phone, she began to have second thoughts about using it as her suspicions grew. Roger insisted that she keep it on her all the time with it turned on. Then it hit her that Roger always seemed to know where she had been and even more what she had been doing.

"Is he able to spy on me by using my phone?" she wondered as she turned it off and tossed it into the trash. She would need to find another way to contact the detective. Then she and Teddy walked out the door of their home for the last time.

Once they were in the car and getting onto I-85 she began to calm down.

"Where are we going, Mom?" Teddy asked as he looked up from his tablet.

"It's an adventure, so just relax and enjoy the ride," she replied with a smile.

For the next two hours Teddy played his games as Veronica drove as inconspicuously as possible toward Charlotte. Teddy fell asleep and Veronica began to think of how she might approach Detective Williams. It made her begin to wonder why he was about to be "terminated." She was certain that in this case it was not a termination of his employment but his life. She would have to tell him that his life was in danger and that the two of them along with her evidence was what it would take to collapse the whole Organization and save all of their lives.

The next problem that occurred to her was how to get in touch with him. She recalled seeing a cell phone number in his personnel file. She would have to get that number and give him a call when she got to Charlotte. She looked at her GPS and determined that she would get into the Charlotte area around midnight. Maybe she could stop and call sooner but remembered that she had thrown her cell phone in the trash at the condo.

"Great!" she muttered under her breath so as to not wake Teddy. "We'll have to get a hotel room and I can call from the phone in the room."

That made much more sense to her. It would also give her a private place to meet this Williams guy and try to convince him that he was in danger and that they needed to find a way to bring down Percy Brigston's Organization.

CHAPTER 4 • MURDER
IN CHARLOTTE

Roger stepped off the plane as soon as he could. Both pilots greeted him at the bottom of the stairs. He could see a local man waiting by a nondescript car that was already running.

"There will be a change of plans tonight. Be prepared to return to Atlanta on short notice." He said as he lifted both of his bags and walked towards the car.

As he did, the man opened the driver's door. Uncharacteristically of Roger, he did not greet the man but instead tossed his two bags into the passenger's seat before he got behind the wheel, slammed the door shut, and drove away.

He was several miles away from the airport when he reached into his briefcase and found the throwaway phone. He turned it on and found Detective Williams' cell phone number. He called the number and listened as it rang until it went to voicemail. He silently cursed the non-answer but would not leave a message.

Roger drove around the city for the next hour as he pondered how to reach his target. The pressure to get back to Atlanta was building by the second. He pulled into a grocery store parking lot to give himself time to think. It occurred to him that perhaps Williams would be more likely to answer a caller he knew. A smile crept onto his face as he realized that he could start taking care of the second objective of this assignment and reach Williams with one call. He picked up the cell phone and found the number of his main law enforcement resource in Charlotte,

Lieutenant Sidney Jenkins.

"Call the boss at this number ASAP!" he typed and sent a text message.

A moment later the cell phone started to ring.

"Jenkins here," said a deep voice.

"You know who this is?" Roger said quietly.

"Yes sir, what can I do for you?" the voice asked.

"I need to meet with Jeffrey Williams as soon as possible and he is not answering his phone," Roger said calmly.

"I'll find him and have him call you back, sir," the voice said and ended the call.

Roger sat back while waiting for the call and thought about Veronica. She had been his best attempt at finding a way to overcome his addiction. She had been barely eighteen when he seduced her by introducing her to a life of unimaginable wealth and privilege. She had always been petite and could have easily passed for being several years younger than she actually was. Those first few months were some of most exciting he had ever known and even now he had to acknowledge that he had fallen in love with her. Three months later she announced that she was pregnant.

There was a part of him that suspected that Veronica had deliberately become pregnant in an attempt to get him to leave his wife. On the other hand, he was thrilled with the thought of watching his child grow inside his young mistress. Terresa had never been able to conceive, so there was also a desire on his part to have a child to carry on the Culpepper lineage even if it would be of a bastard nature.

That was when he sat her down and explained that she would never be anything more than his mistress. He would support her and see that the child would be cared for. If she did not like that arrangement, then the other alternative would be for him admit that the baby was his child, arrange to be awarded sole custody, and Veronica would be out on her own. That was when their relationship changed from being lovers to her being his kept woman.

Suddenly his reflections were interrupted by the sound of the phone ringing.

"This is Williams," said a voice that was clearly on edge when Roger accepted the call.

"Yes, Jeffrey. I need to meet with you as soon as possible. We are aware of what you have been doing and frankly, we have been impressed by your ingenuity and think we have a more appropriate role for you in The Organization," Roger said and waited to see if the man took his bait.

"I need more money!" Jeffrey Williams growled.

"You will be handsomely rewarded for your new role. In fact, I have one hundred grand for you tonight in cash. I also need to discuss the added responsibilities we will want you to assume," Roger said and waited for the other man to reply.

There was silence for a noticeable period of time.

"Tell me what you want me to do," the man finally said.

"Not on the phone. As a cop you should know that someone might be listening," Roger replied.

"Fine, meet me at South Park Mall in an hour," Williams replied.

"Too many eyes. I will meet you at Neck Road Boat Ramp at ten thirty," Roger replied.

Again Williams seemed to hesitate but then sighed, "Fine, but no tricks!"

Roger ended the call and put the car in drive so that he would be in the area before Williams could get there.

On the way he called Sidney Jenkins.

"It's me," Jenkins said, answering on the first ring.

"Your boy called me. I appreciate your assisting me but there is more we need to discuss in person. Meet me at the Concord Regional Airport at eleven-thirty tonight. I'll arrange for a conference room. Tell them that you are there to meet with me and I will be along shortly," Roger said and ended the call.

Roger made the arrangements to meet with Jenkins and informed the pilots to plan on being wheels up at twelve-thirty.

He drove to the meeting area, which was a public boat ramp

with a large parking lot. There were a few vehicles with trailers indicating that there were people present doing some night fishing. It was very dark and very quiet. He left the parking lot and found a place to watch the other man arrive without being noticed himself. His biggest concern was that Williams would be smart enough not to come alone.

It was not long before an SUV came down the access road. Roger could clearly see that there was only one occupant in the vehicle and most telling, there was no boat or trailer. It had to be Jeffrey Williams. Roger watched the time and when it was nearly ten-thirty, he drove into the parking lot and saw the SUV parked away from all the other vehicles. He pulled up next to the SUV.

He got out of his car and walked to the driver's door and watched as the window lowered and the driver looked up at him.

"Are you Jeffrey Williams?" Roger asked and watched as the man nodded that he was.

"This is for you," Roger said as he held up the heavy gym bag.

Williams grabbed the bag and pulled it into his vehicle. He looked warily at Roger as he unzipped the bag and quickly looked down. He turned on the dome light and suddenly could not believe the cash that was in his hands. He had just pulled out a five-thousand-dollar bundle of hundreds. He was getting ready to fan it to make sure the bundle was what it said it was when he felt a prick in his neck as if an insect had bitten him. He looked up at Roger who watched him closely.

Roger observed the bundle of hundreds fall from Williams's hand. He smiled slightly as he understood that the dirty cop no longer had a sense of touch in his fingers and then quickly realized that his muscles no longer obeyed his brain. His victim continued to look at him with unblinking eyes as Roger put on medical gloves and reached in and unlocked the doors. Roger walked over to the passenger door, opened it, and got in. He pulled the bag of cash back into his possession. He retrieved the bundle that had fallen into Jeffrey's lap and put it back in the bag as well.

Roger searched the man and located his gun, which was

positioned between his thigh and the center console where it could be accessed quickly. Roger also found the other man's cell phone and smiled when he saw that it was audio recording the exchange. He stopped it and deleted the recording. Roger checked the call log and noted that there had been no calls, text messages or emails since their call. He put the phone back where he had found it. He then quickly looked around the vehicle to see if there were any other recording devices. Satisfied that there were none he turned Williams' head and looked into the man's eyes. He could see that Jeffrey was aware of what was happening but his entire body was paralyzed from the effects of the tranquilizer he had injected into Jeffrey's neck as he had fixated on the cash.

Roger checked the time and noted that nearly fifteen minutes had passed since he had injected the tranquilizer. The dose should last for another fifteen minutes before it would wear off. He set a timer on the phone to two minutes before Williams would begin to revive. It was important that the double-crossing cop was able to move when he experienced his heart attack.

"Now we play the waiting game," Roger said to himself as he studied the parking lot, which remained empty of life except for the two men in the SUV.

While he waited, he picked up the detective's gun and put it in the man's holster. He then changed his thoughts back to the situation with Veronica.

"I should have gotten rid of her years ago," he thought with regret. "Perhaps if I had given her some cash and told her it was over she might have gone away quietly. It would not have had to be all that much, probably no more than a million as a palimony settlement with an agreement of non-disclosure regarding my bastard son," he shook his head at the missed opportunity.

Now she would have to die but how could he arrange that in a way so as not to arouse the suspicion of the police or even more importantly, Percy Brigston. It would either need to be an accident or perhaps she could just suddenly disappear. The first would take planning and perhaps time that he did not have and the second might leave nagging questions from the cops. He could always convince Percy that he decided to terminate her due to her getting too old to please him.

The alarm rang on the phone. Roger pulled the vial of potassium chloride and the syringe that he had used earlier. He quickly filled the syringe and reached over and gently slapped Jeffrey Williams face and could see that some feeling was returning to the drugged cop. Then Williams tried to speak but his tongue and mouth refused to form the words. Roger quickly located a vein in Jeffrey's wrist, inserted the needle, and pushed the plunger.

Roger opened the passenger door and gathered the gym bag and did one last careful check for anything that he might be leaving behind in the car. There was nothing but it always paid to be careful. As he walked back around the car he could see Jeffrey beginning to convulse as his heart was out of control. Then with one final jerk, Jeffrey Williams slumped over the wheel of his SUV. Roger reached in and checked the man's pulse and there was none to be found.

Roger got in his car and checked the time. It was just after eleven. It would take just over a half hour to get back to the Concord Airport. So far, his timing had been impeccable. He exited the parking lot and did not see any other cars until he was back on the main road.

Roger arrived as he expected and was quickly admitted to drive the car into the secure area. He gathered his briefcase and gym bag and walked over to the awaiting aircrew.

"I will have a brief meeting in the terminal but when I return, I would like to get back to Atlanta as quickly as we can," he said in his calm, businesslike voice.

"Sure thing Mr. Culpepper. Would you like us to take your bags?" Jimmy asked.

"No thank you, I will need these for my meeting," Roger replied as he turned and walked towards the terminal.

He was directed to the conference room where he found Sidney Jenkins waiting for him. The two men quickly shook hands before taking a seat.

"I trust your meeting with Jeffrey turned out the way you wanted it to?" Sidney asked.

"Actually, that is why I need to meet with you as well. Sometime between now and tomorrow it is going to be discovered that Detective Williams has suffered a fatal heart attack," Roger said as he carefully evaluated Sidney's body language.

"That is such a shame. Not surprising though since he was under such a strain with his gambling debts and marital problems," Sidney replied.

"I am certain that his sudden passing may warrant an investigation. I would not want it to delay the closure that his wife and girlfriend deserve. Perhaps you could make sure the investigation is moved along at an appropriate pace with the correct finding. I believe that this will assist you in getting that done," Roger said as he handed the gym bag to Sidney Jenkins.

The Lieutenant looked into the bag and then back at Roger before saying, "I believe that will be easily arranged."

"Good! This was an extremely unfortunate and unneeded situation. It is important that all of our people understand the consequences if The Organization is threatened. I want you to make sure that all our people in this market are aware of what has happened here. Do we understand each other?" Roger asked as he looked deep into the other man's eyes.

"It will not happen again," Sidney replied as a drop of sweat trickled down his temple.

"Good, I look forward to your complete report next week so that this may be put behind us," Roger said as he stood up, took his briefcase, and walked out the door.

Roger felt good about the results of his visit to Charlotte as he boarded the jet but now he had a much bigger issue to deal with and time was not his ally.

CHAPTER 5 • DECISIONS MADE

Veronica was getting close to Charlotte and she began to think about where she could get a room for the night. She knew that if she used her credit card she would be located by Roger within minutes. She needed to find a place that would accept cash. Perhaps one of those cheap motels would take cash and ask no questions. She looked at each interchange and tried to gage just what kind of a neighborhood it was. Then she saw that the upcoming one was dominated by truck stops, fast food, and other questionable businesses including several run-down motels.

She pulled into the third-rate motel just outside of Charlotte that was called the Express Inn, just before midnight. The cheapness of the hotel made her skin crawl as she walked into the office to see if she could get a room. She saw a man with a food-stained shirt sitting behind the front desk, which was shielded by smudged plexiglass. The man looked up at her as she walked into the office.

"I would like a room for the night," Veronica asked.

The man stood up and looked at her like he was inspecting a piece of meat.

"I need a credit card and your driver's license," the man replied as he studied Veronica.

"I want to pay with cash," Veronica replied.

"Ok, let me have your driver's license," he said as his eyes burned into Veronica.

"Why do you need my driver's license?" Veronica asked.

"Because it is the rules, no driver's license no room!" man said in an annoyed tone.

Veronica began to worry that this might be the story anywhere she would try to find a room. She and her son needed a place to get some sleep and even more important to contact Jeffrey Williams.

"What if we break the rules and you put the money in your pocket?" Veronica asked and hoped that the man's greed would win over his devotion to the rules.

The man looked at her closer and then out at her BMW before asking, "What's your game, lady?"

"My husband and I had a fight and I don't want him to find me," she replied and it was close enough to the truth.

The man seemed to be thinking it over.

Veronica opened her purse and looked in at the bundles of cash. She pulled out three one-hundred-dollar bills and showed them to the night clerk. She slipped the cash through the small slot at the bottom of the plexiglass.

The man was looking her in the eyes as she mouthed the word, "Please."

The man took the money and then handed Veronica an actual key with a large green plastic tag that said "129" in faded white numbers.

"It's in the back and not visible from the road. You will need to be out by ten in the morning," the clerk said as he took the cash and slipped it into his pants pocket.

Veronica grabbed the key and headed back to her car.

"Just what kind of place have you just checked into?" she silently asked herself as she got back in the SUV and pulled to the backside of the seedy motel.

She gently shook Teddy as she parked in front of the room. He yawned as he looked at her.

"Come on, sweety, we are at a motel for the night." She said as she gathered the gym bag along with her purse and took him to the room.

The room smelled of strong cleaning products as they stepped in. Veronica quickly pulled the curtain closed. Then she set the bag and purse down before she returned to the car to get her bag and Teddy's backpack that held their meager possessions. When she came back in she closed the door, locking and securing it with the old-style safety chain.

"Where are we, Mom?" Teddy asked as he rubbed his eyes and looked around the cheap room with its worn-out furniture and stained carpet.

"It's late, sweetheart. Put on your pjs and get under the covers." Veronica replied.

Teddy changed as Veronica looked at the old telephone that sat on the nightstand. She studied the instructions that were on a sticker on the phone itself. She would need to dial nine to get an outside line. She reached into her own bag and pulled out her laptop. In a few minutes she had Jeffrey Williams' personnel file open and his cell phone number.

She felt Teddy crawl onto the bed with her and she took him into her arms as he snuggled against her. She stroked his hair and then kissed his forehead.

"How did I get so lucky to have such a wonderful little boy?" Veronica wondered as she felt the center of her world slowly drift off to sleep in her arms.

Her mind wandered back to those first few months with Roger Culpepper and how she had been overwhelmed by what being truly wealthy was like. The luxury of five-star hotels, private jets, front row seats for any entertainment event, and rubbing elbows with celebrities and the elites. Shopping at only the finest shops in New York, Beverly Hills, Paris, and anywhere else that he would take her as his arm candy.

He had hired her as his administrative assistant and in addition to her six-figure salary he provided her with a company-owned condominium and company car. Her work, what there was of it, was mostly paying invoices, setting appointments for Roger, and answering the phone. Her real work was seeing to Roger's personal needs and desires.

Veronica had not been so naive as to believe that being Roger Culpepper's mistress was any long-term position. He would kick her out when he no longer wanted her. She worked hard to understand what pleased him in the bedroom or as she discovered, in so many other locations. She could tell that she was being successful and she believed that Roger had truly fallen in love with her.

In those early days she had a secret hope that Roger would leave his wife and that she would become the new Mrs. Roger Culpepper. She had made the decision to forget to take her birth control for a while and then she announced to Roger that they were going to have a baby.

She cringed as she remembered just how badly she had misjudged Roger's reaction to the news. He had calmly explained to her that he would never leave his wife.

"You have two options," he said as he looked at her, "First, you can continue to be my mistress and live the life you have been enjoying but you must raise the child as a single mother. Of course, I will provide for the child but that child will not know that I am the father."

Veronica had been stunned but asked bitterly, "What if I don't want my child to be a bastard?"

"That would bring us to the second option," he said and his voice grew very cold and menacing. "I will admit that I am the father. I will beg Terresa for her forgiveness of my indiscretion which she will gladly give. I will then hire the best attorneys to have you declared unfit to be a parent. I will have Terresa adopt the child and we will raise it as our own. I will then kick you out and you will be back waiting tables with your mother."

Even thirteen years later a chill passed through her as to the absolute certainty of Roger's threat! Veronica held Teddy closer to her.

There was no choice for the eighteen-year-old Veronica. She surrendered whatever was left of her dignity and became Roger Culpepper's kept woman and a single mom. It was then that Roger demonstrated just what kind of a cruel deviant he truly was.

"I will never regret the decision I made," she thought as she kissed her son's brow.

Then she realized that she had made a second decision a few hours before. Again, there was no choice other than the one that she had made. Unfortunately, the risks of her decision would not be just her life but her son's life as well if she did not bring down Roger Culpepper and Percy Brigston. She slipped out of the bed being careful not to disturb Teddy's slumber. She pulled the covers over him as she smiled at the center of her existence.

She picked up the phone and dialed Jeffrey Williams' number. She listened as the phone rang until it went to voicemail. She only hesitated for an instant before hanging up. What she had to say to him had be said in person.

"Perhaps he is asleep. I'll call him again in the morning," She said quietly as she turned out the lights before slipping back into bed.

She again cuddled with her son and she was asleep in an instant.

Veronica opened her eyes as she became aware of the television playing. She looked at the cheap alarm clock and was shocked that it said it was nine-thirty. They needed to be out of the room in thirty minutes. She turned over and saw Teddy flipping through channels. It was then that he landed on a station that had a breaking news alert.

She felt ill when she read, "Charlotte Detective Found Dead."

She took the remote from Teddy and turned up the sound.

"Details are somewhat sketchy at this hour but what we do know is that a body was found here at the Neck Road Boat Ramp parking lot. The man has been identified as Jeffrey Williams, a long time Detective assigned to the Vice Squad of the Charlotte Police Department. Authorities at the scene indicate that there is no evidence of foul play but that a full investigation will be conducted," said the youthful looking reporter as she closed her segment.

Veronica was stunned.

"I'm hungry, Mom," Teddy said.

"We'll get something in a little bit, sweety," she replied as she tried to think about what to do.

Then she had a thought, "I'll call the team that is investigating Williams' death!"

She quickly looked up the number for the Charlotte Police. She dialed the number she had found in the torn telephone book.

"Charlotte Police Department," a woman's voice said.

"I have information about that detective's death, Jeffrey Williams," Veronica said.

"One moment," the voice replied.

Veronica turned on her computer and opened the personnel file for Jeffrey Williams in order to be prepared to answer some questions. She was studying the form when another voice came over the phone.

"Hello, this is Lieutenant Jenkins," a man's voice said.

It was then that her eyes landed on a line on Williams' personnel file that was labeled "Recruited by" and the name "Sidney Jenkins" was in the box. Veronica slammed the phone down.

"Dear God!" she moaned.

"How long before they come here to see who called?" she wondered before she said, "Teddy, we have to leave right away,"

She quickly grabbed their stuff and headed for her car. Within a few minutes they were back on I-85 heading north.

CHAPTER 6 • ROGER
HAS A PROBLEM

R oger had quickly driven back from Brown Field to his office and arrived there just after one thirty in the morning. He walked into the dark office with the faint hope that he had locked his office or had only imagined that he had forgotten to turn off his computer and lock the vault.

As soon as he turned on the lights in Veronica's office, he noticed that his office door was closed and locked tight. His hope soared as he opened the door to his private office. Perhaps he had locked the door when he had left after all. Maybe Veronica never had the opportunity to enter his office and discover what his real business was.

He opened his office and noticed that his computer was off and the camouflaged door to the vault room was closed. Perhaps it had all been his imagination. Relief flooded over him as the tension began to leave his body.

He sat down and turned the computer on. He decided to send a secured message to Percy Brigston on the outcome of his visit to Charlotte. He was just getting into his secured messaging software when he noticed an alert from the computer's security system.

"Have you copied Secured Files to an external drive?" the computer asked.

"Shit!" was the word that came from his mouth.

He quickly ascertained that all of the "Organization" files had been copied onto a thumb drive.

Then his eyes looked to the secret door that led into the vault. He stood uneasily and walked to the door. He released the hidden latch and the door opened. He turned on the lights and could not detect any difference from his previous visit. He went to the vault and put the combination in the lock. The vault door opened silently as the interior lights turned on. Then Roger knew he was in serious trouble.

"Crap!" he swore as he stepped into the vault.

It was obvious that there was a significant amount of United States currency missing. It would take an inventory to be precise but he guessed there was at least three hundred grand missing. He could see the drawer to the storage of diamonds was also slightly open. Each box in that drawer contained over one hundred flawless diamonds that averaged one caret or more or about a quarter of a million dollars per box. He ascertained there was over a million dollars of diamonds missing.

While all of that was important, it was the third drawer that held his attention. He had stopped breathing as he opened the drawer and then groaned as he saw the small foam rubber holder for the thumb drive was empty.

In his fifty years of life, never had he felt such despair as he did at that moment. All of his faith had been placed in that perverse recording of Brigston raping that poor underaged girl. It was his secret insurance policy if Percy had ever decided to sacrifice him or if he ever needed to make a deal if The Organization ever collapsed.

Then he heard the chime that indicated Brigston had just sent him a message. He walked over to the computer and opened the message.

"Has the Charlotte matter been resolved?" the message from Brigston asked.

"Yes, Jenkins will make sure that all lose ends are cleaned up," he replied.

"Most excellent, old man," came the reply.

"I'm going to take the next couple of days off to take care of a personal matter," Roger typed.

"Personal matter?" Brigston asked.

"Just a little situation with Veronica," Roger replied.

"I told you that you should have traded her in for something younger years ago. There's plenty of our product available to scratch your itch with. Do what you need but don't forget about Project Lorelei," Brigston replied.

"No problem. Good night," he typed before he closed the message window.

Roger grimaced as he thought about his situation. He had ten days to deal with Veronica before Project Lorelei would require all of his attention. Percy would grow very suspicious if he were not available to oversee their most valuable project of the year. Lorelei was worth over a quarter of a billion dollars and maybe more. Even more important than the money was the potential for blackmail of several influential men and women who had some rather deviant desires for young girls of northern European origin. They were what was called special order merchandise since they would not go through the normal training process.

Roger knew the clock was running and if he were not successful in terminating Veronica in the next few days then his own life would also be over.

The first order of business was to determine where she was. Hopefully she would not be expecting him back in Atlanta yet. Roger returned to the vault and proceeded to load one bag with cash and another with a supply of tranquilizers, poison, and a broad assortment of other tools to subdue or dispose of people. The last thing he added to the bag was a nine-millimeter pistol with a silencer.

Roger then picked up his cell phone and checked for Veronica's location on an app that he had hidden on her phone. He frowned when he saw that her phone had been turned off but of some value as it had been turned off at the condo. He next checked on her credit card usage. The last charge was for gas at a gas station just a few blocks from the office. Then he checked to see what calls she had made and if she had any text messages or emails. There was only one call and that was to the nanny, which confirmed that Teddy must be with her.

As he set down his phone, he realized that just like he had been tracking Veronica by her phone, he was also leaving an electronic trail. There was no doubt that he would come under scrutiny given his long relationship with her. He put his phone on his desk on its charger. He then went to the vault and got another phone that could not be traced to him but was the mirror image of his own phone. He also picked up an envelope which contained a false identity for him with credit cards that matched.

"I'll have to go to her condo to check if she is there. If she is not then I will be able to pick up my ace in the hole," he calculated as he closed up the office and walked to his car.

He arrived at the high-rise condominium about twenty minutes later. He went to the elevator and was quickly trying to develop a plan on what he would do if Veronica was at the condo. The only thing he could think of was suicide by tossing her off the balcony. As the elevator door opened, he felt sick to his stomach about what he had to do. Then it hit him that Teddy was also at the condo!

"Can I really kill my own son?" he asked himself but he already knew that he would do whatever it took to protect the most important person, who was obviously himself.

At the door he stopped and listened for any sign of activity.

"Maybe the boy will be asleep," he thought to himself. "If I slip in quietly maybe I can take care of her in her sleep. A little young for a heart attack but with enough money and the right coroner it might be pulled off," Roger thought as he opened the door and slipped into the luxury condo.

He silently made his way to Veronica's bedroom and to his disappointment her bed was empty. He shook his head as he walked toward Teddy's bedroom. If they were there it would be painful but necessary to kill them both.

When he carefully opened the door he looked into yet another unoccupied bedroom. He felt both relief and disappointment as he stood there. Still, he realized that he had no choice and this was just a delay in resolving a problem that had to be dealt with.

Roger walked back to Veronica's bedroom and then to her closet. He noticed that the safe was open and its contents were gone.

"At least she is smart enough to get everything she can while she can," he said to himself but quickly added, "Not that it will make any difference."

Roger was not after the safe or its contents but instead reached up on the highest shelf and brought down a small electronic device that had a blank screen. He held down two different buttons and the screen came to life. Roger scrolled through options and then frowned.

"They're both stationary near Charlotte," he said a little mystified as he wondered why they would be there.

He briefly thought of calling and having his plane prepped to return to Charlotte but decided that it would be best if he travelled by car to limit any record of his being in the area where Veronica and Teddy would have to be dealt with. He also needed time to think about how he would kill them and four hours on the road would help in doing that.

Roger looked at his phone's contact list, found the number he wanted, and hit call.

The phone was on its fourth ring when a groggy voice said, "This better be good or I'm going to kick your ass."

"This is Roger," he said calmly and then he heard the sharp inhale of breath on the other end of the call.

"Sorry, boss. I didn't see who was calling. What do you need?" the man asked as he tried to gather his sleep-addled wits.

"I need a car, something that blends into traffic but that can go off-road. Also, I want it to not be traceable to anyone connected with The Organization," Roger said.

"I can take care of that. When do you want it?" the man asked.

"At my office in thirty minutes," Roger answered.

"No can do, boss. The car is over an hour away and that is the closest that I have. Let's see, it's three-forty...hmm...I can have it to your office and gassed by six," the man said.

Roger thought about it and while he wanted to get moving, he could also feel the exhaustion from the last twenty-four hours so he said, "Make it nine and put a tarp, rope, shovel, and pick in the back."

"You got it, boss." The man said as Roger ended the call.

He took one last look around the condo and then left.

Back at the office he changed clothes from his business casual to jeans, golf shirt, and a pair of hiking boots. His mind was already pulling a basic plan together. His overall objective was to permanently eliminate Veronica. He also needed to recover the insurance video and the copied files from his computer. He would need to know if she had shared any of the information with someone else. That was particularly true of the video. Finally, it would be nice to recover the diamonds and cash. He knew there was a good million in diamonds missing and probably between three and five hundred thousand in cash.

Based on those objectives, he determined that he would have to take Veronica alive. He would need to find out what she had done with the things she took and potentially whom she may have talked to or shared the information with. That also meant that he would need to kidnap Teddy as well. In fact, Teddy could be very helpful in making her talk.

No matter what, they would have to die. Roger was a consummate strategist so he began to consider what would be the consequences of Veronica and Teddy being found dead. Since he was unsure where he would catch up with them, he could not rely on having local resources to ensure that an appropriate "case closed" was reached. No matter what, it would be critical to keep suspicion from being directed at him or The Organization.

Unfortunately, there was no doubt that he would be the subject of scrutiny no matter how he dealt with Veronica. Suicide would be the easiest for just her but Teddy would need to be killed as well. Again, Roger felt exhausted. He lay down on the couch and set his alarm for eight-thirty. He continued to think about his options until sleep overwhelmed him.

CHAPTER 7 • MOUNTAINS, MOONSHINE, & GHOSTS

S am Stone opened his eyes to find his dog, Diesel, looking at him. Diesel was a mix of black lab and rottweiler. He had just turned two years old and weighed in at one-hundred-and-twenty pounds of pure muscle that was utterly devoted to his master. Sam, on the other hand, considered the dog his best friend and a far better conversationalist than ninety percent of the people he had ever met in his sixty years on earth.

Sam reached out and rubbed the ears on the dog's massive head. The dog seemed to smile back at him. This was their morning routine.

"I take you're ready for your morning constitutional?" Sam asked as Diesel's tail whipped back and forth in affirmative answer to the question.

Sam sat up on the bed and reached down for his bib-overalls that lay alongside the bed. He quickly pulled them on and walked to the door that opened out to the parking area of his mountain home. Diesel happily bounded off down the drive and occasionally stopped to sniff at something that drew his attention. Then he found just the right tree and lifted his leg. Sam walked over to the edge of the woods and stopped to look around.

"I think I will join you," he said as he opened his fly.

Sam allowed Diesel to continue to explore as he looked over the homestead that he had carved out of the mountains here in Mitchell County, North Carolina. His property was close to fifty acres set well back into the wilderness. His house sat at the top of a ridge with a magnificent view. Not far from the house there was a spring that flowed out of the side of the mountain. It was the source of the water for his house and business. The spring water ran down the hillside where it emptied into a larger stream that spilled over a waterfall before continuing to the South Toe River. Sam could hear the sound of the waterfall and was reassured that all was well with the world.

"Come on, Diesel, we have a busy day today," he said as he stepped up on the porch and opened the door before his dog bounded past him into the house.

The next order of business for the day was coffee for him and food for the dog. Sam started the coffee and then poured a generous amount of food into Diesel's bowl. The dog sat and waited until Sam stood back up and pulled out an apple and a granola bar from the pantry.

Sam then bowed his head and if another person had been there, they would have observed that the massive dog seemed to join him as he prayed. "Father, we thank you for this food and all of your wonderful blessings. We pray, Lord, that you will make this a good day. Amen!"

After the prayer ended, Diesel devoured his food as Sam poured himself a cup of coffee and walked out onto the upper deck. He set his food and coffee down on the table next to his chair. He inhaled deeply and savored the clean mountain air. Then he sipped his coffee and felt the caffeine rush into his blood.

Diesel, having finished his food, came out and lay down by Sam.

Sam closed his eyes and the ghosts came to gather around him. When he had first moved to the mountains he had hoped that they would not follow him. They did but now nearly eight years later he had found a peace with them instead of the terror of their accusations. Sam understood that their deaths were on his hands. He freely admitted his guilt to them and he felt it was only fair they should now find life with him here on his mountain.

He opened his eyes as he pulled out a pocket knife, sliced the apple, and ate it while he continued to drink the strong black coffee in his thermal cup. His mind settled on today's task. He would travel to Greensboro to get his business supplies. He would make a stop in McDowell County along the way to make a delivery and collect this month's income.

Sam needed the income as it was what he lived on. He took pride that he had used the small inheritance from his parents to buy the land he lived on and the materials he had used to build his house. His expenses were small and he lived off the grid for the most part. His electricity came from a hydro-generator. He kept a garden for vegetables that he ate when in season and canned the excess for the winter. He also hunted and fished on a regular basis, which supplemented his own livestock source of chickens and pigs. Even the apple was from an old orchard that had come with the land he had purchased.

He closed his eyes and the ghosts gathered closer to him and one of them who looked like a young girl spoke, "There is always the other money. It is alright to spend it."

"No! It's blood money," Sam said quietly.

The other money was his savings and pension money that was in a bank account that he vowed he would never touch. Sam had a long career with the United States government but he tried not to think about those days.

He finished his coffee while eating the granola bar.

"Time to get this show on the road," he said to Diesel as he got up and went into the house.

He cleaned up the few dishes that he had used and then went into the bedroom and made the bed. Next, he went and showered and put on clean clothes. He looked at himself in the mirror and smiled as he knew that people who had known him before his escape to the mountains would have a hard time recognizing him. He was just under six feet tall with a build that would be described as average. His hair was a salt-and-pepper grey, which included his long beard. When he was wearing his overalls and black cowboy hat he looked like a true mountain man.

His next chore was to go out to feed the chickens and collect their eggs. He had found the easiest way to do this was throw some food on the ground and while the hens and the rooster were distracted, he quickly gathered the eggs. After, he put more food into the feeder and filled their water trough. Next he went over and fed his two pigs in their pen.

He went out to the garage and opened the back of his old-style Ford Bronco. He then walked over to the other side of the garage where he opened a secret door. On the inside were boxes of quart jars. Sam loaded eight cases of jars filled with an amber liquid into the back of his truck and closed the secret door before going back to the house.

He reached into a drawer and pulled out a nine-millimeter pistol that he slid into an inner pocket of his overalls. He then pulled out a large stiletto knife, flicked the release, and watched the double-edged blade shoot out of the metal handle. The edges were razor sharp.

"Always pays to be prepared," he said as he retracted the blade before slipping it into his pocket and picking up his cell phone as he left the house.

"You're in charge, Diesel," he said as he started the old Bronco and headed down the drive.

He drove down to the entrance to the Blue Ridge Parkway at Little Switzerland. Shortly after getting on the Parkway he passed through the Little Switzerland Tunnel while enjoying the beauty of his chosen home. After a few more miles, he went by the overlook for Table Top and marveled at the majesty of the view. Many times he had stopped and took a few minutes to admire that view but today he had an appointment to keep.

Just a few miles further was a road that exited the Parkway, which turned into Altapass Highway, but there was another road that passed back under the Parkway that became Peppers Creek Road and would take those that knew about it back down the mountain to Marion. This was the road that Sam headed down. In just a couple of miles he saw a red Chevy pickup parked alongside the road. He stopped nearby and watched as a thirty-year-old man stepped out of the Chevy.

"How are you doing, Richard?" Sam asked as he got out of the Bronco.

"Doing well!" the other man replied.

"I got your twenty-four gallons for you," Sam said as he pointed in the back of his Bronco.

"You got a little sample for me?" Richard asked hopefully.

Sam pulled a pint jar out from under the seat and handed it to his customer. The other man took the top off and sipped the amber liquid.

"Your 'shine gets better every time I taste it," the man said as he rolled his eyes.

"Glad you like my Toe River Rye," Sam replied with a chuckle.

"All you got is twenty-four gallons?" Richard asked with disappointment while Sam nodded yes, "You know I could move twice as much if you would make it. This will all be sold in a couple of days," Richard added.

Sam smiled at being the only source of aged 'shine. He had learned that by cutting up some oak and charring it he could "age" his liquor. If he moved it in and out of the refrigerator for about a month, he would have rye whiskey that tasted like it had been aged for five years or more.

"I'd need to build a bigger still but I'll think about it," Sam replied. "You got the money?"

Richard pulled a thick envelope from his back pocket and handed it to Sam. Sam opened it and thumbed the cash. He had no doubt that Richard would never shortchange him and that there were forty-three-hundred dollars in the envelope.

It only took the two of them a few minutes to transfer the moonshine and for the two vehicles to leave headed in different directions.

Sam smiled as he headed on down the mountain to get to I-40 and then on to Greensboro. He started thinking that perhaps now was the time to expand his operation.

CHAPTER 8 • PANIC, PARANOIA, & PANCAKES

Veronica was nearly hysterical as she drove her luxury SUV on I-85 passing through the heart of Charlotte.

"Everything that I tried has failed! Jeffrey Williams is dead! Then I tried to reach the head of the team investigating his death and it is a man who works for Roger!" she thought as she fought the urge to throw herself on the ground, curl into a ball and cry.

"I'm hungry," Teddy said as he looked out the window.

His comment snapped Veronica out of her hysteria. She realized that if she panicked, they were both as good as dead. She began to focus on the road and noticed that there was a sizable interchange coming up in a mile labeled "Concord Mills." There seemed to be a significant number of businesses at the end of the off ramp, so she decided that would be the place to get Teddy something to eat and give herself some time to figure out what to do next.

As she pulled to the top of the ramp, she saw there was a coffee-shop-style restaurant with a sign that said they had the best pancakes in North Carolina. The parking lot was filled with cars so the food must be good.

"How about pancakes?" she asked Teddy and he made a happy noise while nodding his head in enthusiastic agreement.

Veronica pulled the car into the lot and saw an open spot about halfway towards the back. She noticed that there was the wall of an adjoining business that the spot backed up against.

She backed the car in so that the license plate would not be visible to anyone driving through the parking lot.

"Are the cops looking for me?" she wondered to herself but decided there was no sense in taking chances.

She was tempted to grab the gym bag and take it with them as they started to get out of the car but thought that might look a little odd to someone. She determined that it was better to leave everything in the car except for her purse. She did make sure that the car was locked as they started across the parking lot.

They walked into the crowded restaurant where a middle-aged woman greeted them. "Just the two of you?"

"Yes, please," Veronica said and was surprised when the woman picked up two menus and led them to a booth.

They both looked at the menus, which were divided into breakfast and lunch selections. Veronica had thought she would never be able to eat but as she looked at the menu and smelled the aroma of the food being consumed all around her, she felt her stomach rumble to remind her she had not eaten since lunch the day before.

"Hi, my name is Patty. What can I get you to drink?" said an older woman in a waitress uniform that reminded Veronica of her mother.

"I'll have coffee," Veronica said as she looked up at the waitress before looking at her son.

"Can I have a coke?" he asked his mother.

"I think you better have a glass of milk. You can have a coke later," Veronica said as she rolled her eyes at her boy.

"I'll have your drinks right out," the older woman said as she walked away.

"So, what are you going to have to eat? As if I did not know already," Veronica asked with a smile.

"Pancakes!" Teddy said eagerly.

Teddy loved pancakes for breakfast and Veronica could swear that the boy would eat his weight in them if she let him.

Patty returned and put a coffee cup in front of her, poured coffee into it, and set the carafe next to the cup. Next a large glass of milk was set in front of Teddy. The waitress then reached into her apron and pulled out a handful of creamers for Veronica and a straw for Teddy.

"Are you ready to order?" Patty asked pleasantly as she looked at the boy.

"I'll have pancakes, please," he asked politely.

"Would you like sausage or bacon with that?" the waitress asked as she wrote his order down.

"Sausage, please," he replied and Veronica could see Patty smile at her son who obviously had been brought up to be polite and respectful.

"I'll have the Denver omelet, lightly cooked, and wheat toast," Veronica said as the waitress turned her attention to her.

"You have your choice of home fries or grits with that," Patty said as she wrote the order on her pad.

"Grits will be fine," Veronica replied.

With their orders completed, Veronica began to ponder just what she should do now. The first thing that was obvious was that she could not stay in Charlotte or return to Atlanta. It was clear that Roger had plenty of people working for him in both cities.

"How far does his reach go?" she wondered to herself.

She had no doubt that she needed to find a place where she and Teddy would be safe until she could figure out a way to get her evidence into the hands of someone not in Roger's or Percy Brigston's pockets. Those pockets had to be deep. They would have to be for them to move their victims around the country. Then it hit her that the one file she opened had said that the girl was from some foreign country.

"My God! They move people internationally!" she said to herself in disbelief.

Her mind reeled at the extent to which their criminal enterprise must reach. She would be in danger just about anywhere she went.

Her thoughts were interrupted when a plate with her omelet appeared in front of her. She looked up to see a plate of pancakes being placed in front of Teddy, who was licking his lips.

Patty completed placing the food on the table before she asked, "Do you need anything else?"

Veronica shook her head as she picked up her fork as she watched her son pour maple syrup on his pancakes with delight. She continued to watch with a warm smile on her face as he began to devour the fluffy stack. Then she started on her omelet, which was cooked to perfection.

For the next ten minutes mother and son focused on their food. It was only when she was nearly finished that Veronica became aware that the table next to their booth had new occupants and her heart skipped a beat when she noticed that they were deputy sheriffs.

"How are your meals?" Patty asked as she walked up to the table.

Veronica was startled by the unseen waitress since her eyes had been locked on the deputies. Her reaction to the question drew the attention of the two law enforcement officers. It felt like their eyes were burning into her as if trying peer into her inner thoughts.

"I'm sorry, I did not mean to surprise you!" Patty apologized.

"My fault, I was just lost in my own thoughts." Veronica said as she began to regain her composure.

"Well, I was asking how your meals were but since they are nearly gone, they must have been good," the waitress said with a chuckle. "Would you like anything else?" she added.

"No, just the check," Veronica said with a smile but her eyes darted toward the two deputies who had resumed their own conversation.

The waitress tore the check from her pad and laid it on the table.

Veronica wanted to grab the check and her son and leave immediately but she realized that would just call more unwanted attention to herself. She tried to calm herself as she continued to be aware that those two deputies were just a few feet away.

"Are they in the pay of Roger? Are they here to keep us under surveillance?" she wondered in her paranoid panic before a more rational thought entered her mind, "They are probably just here to eat."

She then watched as Teddy took the last bite of pancake with obvious relish. She smiled as his eyes looked up at her with total satisfaction.

"Those pancakes must really be the best in North Carolina," a male voice of one of the deputies said with a chuckle.

Veronica looked to see both deputies smiling at Teddy as they admired his appetite for his breakfast.

"I take it you would recommend that we give those pancakes a try," the older of the two deputies said with a smile to Teddy before he turned and looked at Veronica. "He reminds me of my boy. He could eat me out of house and home," he said to her.

"Yes, he's a good eater," Veronica replied with a smile.

The two lawmen then turned back to their own conversation again.

"Are you ready to go?" she asked Teddy, who was wiping his mouth with his napkin.

Veronica stood up and picked up the check as Teddy stepped out of the booth. She was just getting ready to walk away when she heard, "Don't forget your purse, ma'am."

She looked to the older deputy pointing back to where she had been sitting a moment before.

"Oh, thank you!" she said as she reached back and picked up her purse.

It was then that she remembered that she needed to pay in cash so she looked into her bag and saw that she had bundles of hundred-dollar bills as well as a box filled with diamonds. She wondered just how much the contents of her purse were truly worth. Then she saw some of loose bills that she had taken from her safe in the condo. One of those bills was a ten which she pulled out and left on the table as a tip.

Veronica wanted to rush out of restaurant but deliberately reminded herself to walk calmly to the cashier. The cashier looked surprised when Veronica gave her a hundred to pay the eighteen-dollar-and-twenty-seven-cent check. A moment later the cashier handed her back the change.

They returned to the car and it occurred to Veronica again that she had no idea as to where she was going to go next. The one thing she knew for a certainty was that she could not trust any cops. Those two deputies were very likely decent and honest men but her next interaction with law enforcement might be disastrous if they were in the control of The Organization.

"How can you tell the good guys from the bad?" she wondered and then she realized that she had a list of who the bad guys were!

She needed to find a place to look at those files she had copied so that she would know where it was safe to go. She put the car in gear and left the restaurant parking lot. Her first stop was a gas station to fill up and to use the rest rooms, as she had been hesitant to spend any more time at the restaurant. She picked up a couple of cokes and some snacks before she paid the clerk with another hundred and was glad to get back more small bills.

"Is there a park nearby?" she asked after receiving her change.

"Yes, ma'am, Dorton Park is just a few miles up the road," the clerk said and then gave her directions to the park.

Ten minutes later they pulled into the parking lot. Veronica noticed that there was a small covered pavilion beside the playground. There were a few other people around but not too many. This was just what she needed. Teddy could get some physical activity in as she tried to figure out where to go.

"Honey, Mommy needs a little time to do some work on her computer. Why don't you play while I do that?" she explained to Teddy who was looking over at the playground and the other kids.

"Okay!" he said enthusiastically.

Veronica locked the car as Teddy ran off to the playground and the other kids. She found a picnic table at the pavilion where she could see both the car and Teddy as he played. She opened the computer and inserted the thumb drive. She selected the personnel file directory and noticed there was a search option and when she clicked on it there was a choice by geography. Clicking on this there was a choice by country. She clicked on the United States and was next asked to select a state. She picked North Carolina. A map came up of North Carolina by county. She noticed that certain counties were shaded red. Mecklenburg was one of those red counties and that was where Charlotte was located.

"Go red and you are dead," she said quietly to herself.

She noticed that most red areas were along interstate highways and unfortunately for her she was in the middle of where many of those were concentrated. I-85 would take her next to Greensboro but then the red corridors veered either to the east or west before going north again. Her eyes landed on a town about a half an hour due north of Greensboro called Reidsville that was not in a red area. She decided that would be the place to go to so that she could make further plans.

Veronica looked to see Teddy and several other children playing together. He was laughing and having a great time. She looked down at her computer to see the time and it was just after twelve-thirty. Teddy was having such a great time it would be a shame to leave so quickly.

"Maybe another hour here won't matter." She thought as she shut the computer down and enjoyed watching her son playing with the other children.

CHAPTER 9 • ROGER'S CHASE

R oger was startled from a deep sleep when the alarm on his cell phone went off. He quickly got up and went to his bathroom to clean up. He made a cup of coffee and put it into a to-go cup and then looked out into the parking lot. There was a midsized grey GMC SUV parked in a visitor spot. The vehicle looked like millions of others that traveled every road in North America. It would never attract any attention.

He grabbed the two bags he had prepared the night before and then made sure his office was closed down and locked before he stepped out into the parking lot. The GMC was unlocked and the key was in the ignition. He stowed his gear where he could quickly get at it. He noticed that there was a cell phone holder that would be perfect for holding his tracking device.

Roger had suspected that the day might come when he would need to track his mistress or son down. He had taken the precaution of putting tiny transmitters in a number of their possessions, such as her wallet and Teddy's tablet. They were about two-inch squares which were about a thirty-second of an inch thick and weighed a fraction of an ounce. They had a self-contained battery that could last for ten days before they needed charging. He had developed a routine of changing them out once a week.

"Poor little Veronica, you have no idea just how easy this will be," he said as he started the car and headed towards Charlotte.

Once he was out of the Atlanta area he began to think again of the best way to get rid of Veronica and Teddy. A violent death was sure to be investigated and he would be high up the persons of interest list. It was well known in Atlanta that the two of them were more than just employer and employee. Suicide would not work with Teddy being a second victim. Natural causes would also not work since there were two of them. Then there was a chime from the tracker that made him jump.

"Get a grip on yourself!" he said aloud as he hated feeling like he was not in total control.

He looked at the screen and could see that Veronica was getting onto I-85 and going north. He determined that he was about three hours behind her. He thought about calling Sidney Jenkins to pull them in but he didn't want The Organization involved.

That would be an even a bigger problem for Roger than any investigation by law enforcement. He had to keep this quiet until it was over. Percy Brigston did not want anyone connected directly to him to attract undesirable attention. Percy had many enemies and they were always looking for a weak link in the armor that protected his empire.

Percy had many ways of managing his empire. There were thousands of law enforcement officers at every level around the world that were on the payroll but for every cop he owned there were thousands that he did not. Percy also had many government officials in his pocket either as a result of bribes or more often blackmail but again there were those that he did not control and often they were his sworn enemies. Roger also understood just how fast those political elites that they did control would turn on Brigston if the whiff of scandal was ever in the air.

"If Percy ever found out about what has happened, I would be dead. Or if I screw this up and leave a mess, then I will be a suicide victim myself. There is no way that I will ever be able to hide from him. Come on Roger, think!" he said, pressing the gas harder as his anxiety grew.

The tracker chimed again and this time it indicated that Veronica and Teddy were stationary. He could see that they were stopped at an interchange just north of Charlotte. They just sat there as the minutes passed.

"That's it, baby. Just let me catch up to you," he said to his intended victim as the distance diminished.

He went back to his problem and he thought, "Perhaps an accident could be arranged. The tragic death of a young mother and her son could be a cover that would be plausible and not direct attention to me."

"No that won't work unless I have Organization people involved and that will make Percy look at why I had to do such a thing. I don't want that question directed at me," he said as a chill ran down his back.

"Too bad I can't just make them disappear," he said.

That was when things started to come together in his head. He would make them disappear. He would disclose to the police that he had been the victim of a financial fraud committed by his longtime employee.

"Yes, that's good! She used her feminine charms to gain access to those diamonds my customer had entrusted to me. Then she and those diamonds disappeared," he said as a smile spread on his face.

The cops would be looking for a fugitive with access to vast financial resources to elude them with. On the other hand, he could tell Brigston that he had discovered her theft, killed her and unfortunately her son, but had recovered the stolen diamonds. He would have the bodies cremated by one of The Organization's disposal units.

"Yes, that will work! Heck, we can even file an insurance claim and make an extra million. Old Percy will love that!" Roger laughed as he continued to close the gap to Veronica.

Sometime later, the tracking device indicated that his quarry was on the move again. This time they only went a few miles. He noticed that the location was a city park.

"What are you doing?" he wondered but on the other hand the distance was closing rapidly.

His biggest fear was that Veronica was meeting with someone and sharing the records that she had copied. Cold fear gripped him yet once again.

"That would be catastrophic but let's not dream up problems until they happen," Roger said to himself.

Roger tried to focus on driving as fast as he could without getting caught for speeding. Finally he saw that he was only about five minutes from Veronica's location. He was becoming excited and was already running scenarios through his head on how he would abduct her and Teddy without attracting undue attention. Suddenly the tracking device chimed again. They were leaving the park.

"God dammit!" he swore but then he noticed she was getting on I-85 going north again.

Roger looked intently at the cars coming on to the interstate just a little over mile ahead and then he saw the BMW with Veronica and Teddy merge into traffic. He smiled. He now had them in visual range and all he needed was the right opportunity to grab them both!

CHAPTER 10 • ABDUCTION

Veronica and Teddy were just coming into Greensboro and she knew that she, at least, needed a restroom break again. She saw an interchange coming up and with a fast-food joint near the end of the ramp. She turned off the highway and drove the car into the parking lot.

"I need to use the bathroom. How about you?" she asked.

"No, I'm fine. Can I stay in the car?" he asked as he continued to be engrossed in whatever game he was playing on his tablet.

"That's fine. I'll be just a couple of minutes," she said as she got out of the car and headed inside.

Several hundred yards away, Sam Stone was loading six bags of grain into the back of his old Bronco. Each bag weighed fifty pounds and contained either malted rye or flaked corn that along with the one-hundred-and-eighty pounds of sugar would make some fine 'shine.

"Time to get the hell out of civilization and back to where a man can breathe," he said as he closed the back door of the Bronco.

Sam climbed behind the wheel and started the engine. That was when the ghost appeared in the seat beside him. Needless to say, Sam was more than a little surprised. First, there was never just one of them when they came and second, he had never seen one with his eyes open before.

Ghosts had been a part of his life for a long time. He had made his peace with them but in the early days that had not been so. In those early years, the ghosts would one by one recount how Sam had been involved in their violent deaths. He had actually taken the lives of some of them while with others he had caused the circumstances that had led to their deaths. It had been as if he were on trial. After moving to the mountains, he had a night where their accusations became too much and he confessed his guilt to them and begged for their forgiveness.

It was then that a peace came over him that surpassed his mortal understanding and after that there were no more accusations. These days the ghosts still came but they seemed to just want to be there. He did more talking to them than they did to him. When they did talk, they spoke words of encouragement and reassurance.

The ghost that now sat in his passenger seat looked at him and Sam knew who he was or at least who he had been. He was dressed in military fatigues that were filthy and bloodstained. His head was wrapped with a bloody bandage that masked the fatal headwound that had ended his life.

"Good afternoon, Cap," the ghost said.

"Afternoon, Higgins. Is there something I can do for you?" Sam asked as the Bronco's engine idled and his heart pounded.

"We have forgiven you," Higgin's ghost said as he looked ahead through the windshield.

"I know and I am thankful," Sam replied quietly.

"Then why do you not let us go?" the ghost asked as he turned to look at Sam.

"What do you mean? I'm not keeping you," Sam replied and felt truly mystified.

"Yes, you are. You have not forgiven the one person who holds us," the ghost said and seemed to study Sam for a moment before he sadly said, "You must forgive yourself!"

Sam was speechless at first but then mumbled, "I do not deserve forgiveness."

"Perhaps you would be inclined to extend forgiveness to yourself if you were to perform an act of penance," the ghost said and smiled as he again turned and looked through the windshield.

"Penance?" Sam whispered.

"Innocent blood is about to be shed. You are the right man in the right place to stop that from happening. Over there in that parking lot, a young mother and her son are about to be abducted. They will both die this afternoon unless you choose to intervene," the ghost said and then turned to Sam again and said, "Let us go." Sam watched as Higgins faded away.

A tear dripped from Sam's right eye as he put the Bronco in drive and headed towards the parking lot of the fast-food restaurant. He parked his Bronco in the parking lot of the strip mall adjoining the burger joint but far enough away to not be noticed. It was a perfect observation point where he would be able to watch for the abduction of a woman and a boy.

Roger discreetly followed Veronica into the parking lot. He parked just far enough away to go unnoticed as she got out of the car and went into the fast-food restaurant. He knew this was the opportunity that he had hoped for. He grabbed his bag with his murder tools. He quickly filled a syringe with tranquilizer. He then slipped the pistol with its silencer into the back of his pants. He opened the door to the car and walked toward Veronica's car and Teddy.

He came from the back of the BMW on the passenger's side. The window was down and Teddy was busy playing a game on his tablet. Roger quickly poked the needle into his arm and pushed the tranquilizer into the boy.

Roger knew that Teddy only felt a quick sting on his arm like a biting insect before the numbness began to flow through his body. The boy would be aware of everything that was happening around him but would be unable to command his body to do anything.

Roger then opened the rear door to the SUV and he quickly

laid down on the back seat and waited for Veronica to return. This was all going much better than he could have planned. Maybe there was something to be said for playing it by ear.

Sam watched as the man stepped out of the grey SUV and instead of heading toward the entrance of the burger joint, he walked behind the other parked cars until he came to a BMW SUV with a boy sitting in the front passenger seat. Then in the blink of an eye he saw the man jab a syringe into the boy's shoulder.

"Son of a bitch!" he said as he reached to put the Bronco into drive.

Even as the transmission engaged, he watched as the man opened the rear passenger door and disappear into the back seat. Sam was ready to intervene but then he began to think about what he had been told. Mother and son were to be abducted and killed later. He knew that he had no intel on who the bad guy or guys were. He needed to make sure whatever he did was not going to get the woman and her son killed anyway. He needed to know more.

Then he saw an attractive young woman exit the restaurant and walk directly toward the BMW.

Veronica stepped out of the restaurant and could see that Teddy was in the car with his head down.

"That boy loves to play his games," she thought. "He has no idea how much danger we are in. I must get us both somewhere that it is safe, period. Just another hour and we should be able to get a room where I can figure out what to do next."

She opened the door and got in behind the wheel and started to say something to Teddy when she saw he looked like he was sick. She reached over and put her hand on his face and she could see he was awake but it was like he was paralyzed.

"Oh God! What's wrong, baby!" she screamed as she was on verge of going hysterical.

"He'll be alright as long as you do what you are told," Roger's voice said from behind her head.

Veronica instantly looked into the rearview mirror and saw Roger in the back seat and he had a gun in his hand. She felt the world cash down on her and was certain that she was about to die.

"Put the car in drive. We need a quiet place where we can have a little discussion," Roger said but the gun was now pointed at the back of Teddy's seat.

She started the car and pulled out of the parking lot. As they left the shopping center that the burger joint was in, they came to a stop light.

"Turn right," Roger said calmly.

Sam had watched as the mother panicked when she got a good look at her son. The bad guy sat up and must have made himself known because Sam could see the sheer terror on her face. He had no doubt that the woman knew who the man in back seat was.

"So far only one perpetrator but let's see if there are more around before we step in," he said as he watched the BMW pull out of the parking lot and begin to leave the shopping center.

As the car reached the stoplight the right turn signal came on. Sam scanned the surrounding area and could see no one else getting ready to leave or watching.

"OK, just the one. Now I just need to get them isolated so I can get them back and neutralize the asshole." Sam said as he watched the BMW turn on to Holden Road.

He gave them a little time before he began to follow them at a discreet distance.

Roger tried to remain calm but he had never killed someone that he knew personally before. There was no doubt in his mind that they both had to die but the thought of looking into their eyes as he blew their brains out made him feel ill.

Soon after the car had made the right turn, he felt sure that he had made the correct decision as the road passed over an interstate highway and led away from Greensboro. They quickly entered an area where there were tracts of woods and scattered houses.

"Now I just need to find an isolated spot to do what has to be done," he thought to himself.

Then the road moved through another area that was filled with small businesses. He knew he needed to get father away from town. There was a sharp turn to the left before the road came to a dead end at a T-intersection.

"Turn right," he said as again he felt panic that he may have made the wrong choice of roads.

The road once again became more rural and he began to relax but there was still too much traffic so he began to look for an even smaller road. He saw one coming up to the left.

"Turn left," he said and noticed that Veronica was crying as she drove the car.

"I have to keep her calm," he thought.

"Just relax. I just need to know what you have done with the things you took and whom you have talked to. If you are honest with me and give me back what you took then I will get you some money and you and Teddy can just disappear to someplace safe," he said and hoped that Veronica would latch onto the hope that he would let her go with her son.

She continued to sob and he knew she was not yet convinced. He needed her cooperation to make sure he knew the absolute truth as to whom she might have given information to. In particular he needed to know whom she might have met with in

Charlotte.

"Percy Brigston is a dangerous man. If he knew what you have done, we would both be dead and so would Teddy. The only way out of this is for me to make this all go away. To do that, I have to have everything you took back and then I must deal with anyone you might have shared the information with," Roger paused and then added, "You know I would never harm Teddy," he said.

He noticed there was a high school on the right side but dense woods to the left and what appeared to be a little used road going into the woods. It would be perfect.

"Turn into the woods and we can talk about how we are getting out of this," he said as he prepared himself for what was going to happen.

As they started into the woods, he noticed a sign that said the place was "Saferight Nature Preserve."

CHAPTER 11 • MIRACLE

Sam followed the BMW by just managing to keep it in sight. When the BMW started to go by a high school it suddenly hit the brakes hard and then made a sharp left into the woods. It would have been too obvious if he had tried to follow them, so as he passed where they had turned, he looked and saw it was obvious that the road was a dead end. Frankly the perfect place for murder.

He noticed that there was an entrance to the school parking lot just ahead on the right and he would be able to keep his eyes on where the BMW had gone. Sam wanted to make sure that this was not just a ploy to see if they were being followed.

Sam waited for just a couple of minutes before he got out and crossed the road and went into the woods. He quickly located a spot where he could observe the BMW and the three people in it.

"What did you do to Teddy, you bastard?" Veronica asked as she again looked at her son who had his eyes open but his body was as loose as a bowl of jello.

"He'll be fine. I just gave him a tranquilizer. He is quite aware of what we are saying, by the way, so perhaps we should step out of the car," Roger said as he pressed the gun to the back of her head.

They both got out of the car and Roger looked around. He could still see the road they had turned off and part of the school across the street. It was distant but he did not like even the remotest possibility that someone might see him holding a gun on Veronica.

"Move up the trail and then you can tell me all that I need to know so that I can let you and Teddy go," he said as he gave her a little push in the back.

Veronica wanted to believe that Roger would let them go but she knew there was little chance of that happening. It had been a long time since she had prayed but it was all that she could think of to do.

"Please, Lord! Save us!" she pleaded silently as they walked along.

"That's far enough," Roger said quietly as he looked back down the trail and could no longer see any sign of the car, let alone the road or school.

Veronica turned to face him and knew that time was running out for a miracle.

"Where is the stuff you stole from the vault?" Roger asked as he lowered the gun toward the ground.

Veronica remained silent and she could see the anger build on Roger's face.

So could Sam Stone, who had bypassed the trail that Roger and Veronica had arrived on and instead had moved silently through the thick brush with the skills of the hunter that he was. He was only about five paces from them as Roger began to question the woman.

"Time is short, Veronica! Where is the stuff you took?" he asked again.

"I can't trust you," she said as she cringed since she expected him to slap her.

She was surprised when he instead he just exhaled and then said, "Perhaps we should have Teddy join us."

"He doesn't know anything about this!" she replied in panic.

"But maybe he can help you remember what you did with it. Let's go back to the car," Roger said in a way that warned her that this was her last chance to keep Teddy out of this.

"Promise me that you will not harm Teddy!" Veronica pleaded

as tears streaked her face.

"You know I would never harm my son," he said and hoped that she would tell him what he needed to know.

"There's a gym bag in the car with the money and the diamonds and there is more in my purse," she said with a shudder as she surrendered herself to her fate.

"And the computer files you copied?" he asked with a flat voice.

"In my purse," she sobbed.

"Is that where the thumb drive that you took from the vault is?" he asked as his hopes were rising and then felt relief flood over him as Veronica nodded that it was.

"Did you watch the video?" Roger asked and knew she would say she had and sure enough she had a look of disgust on her face as she remembered what she had seen but then nodded again.

"We are close to being through but I need to know who you met with in Charlotte?" he asked as he felt his victory was near.

"I didn't meet with anyone there," she said and looked up him in confusion.

"You spent the night there and then you spent over two hours in a park just north of there. Are you trying to tell me that you just took a few hours off while you were on the run?" Roger asked and hoped that by him giving details of where she had been while in Charlotte that she would suspect he already knew the answer to his own question but he wanted her to confess the details.

Veronica was indeed surprised at Roger's knowledge of where she had been in last twenty-four hours.

"I went there to try to meet with Jeffrey Williams," she replied and Roger started to put the pieces together.

"Did you call him?" Roger asked and already knew that there was no way that she could have spoken to the now dead detective or his own meeting with him would have never happened.

"I called him from a motel but it went to his voicemail," she said and Roger made a mental note to check with Sidney Jenkins

MICHAEL RODNEY MOORE

to see if there were a call to Williams' cell phone after he had died.

"What time did you try to call him?" Roger asked.

"Some time after midnight, I think," she answered a little perplexed.

"OK, what were you doing at that park?" he asked.

Veronica no longer had any reason to hold back so she said, "I was trying to figure out where I could hide from you and Percy Brigston and then try to destroy you both!"

Sam had been listening intently to the interrogation of the young woman but when he heard the name "Percy Brigston" he felt a cold rage as his own memories flashed through his mind.

"That's the truth!" Veronica said as she looked into Roger's eyes and tried to determine if he would let her and Teddy go but she only saw the uncaring eyes of a shark looking back at her and she knew that she was a dead woman.

Roger was satisfied that he had everything that he needed but now he had to finish the job.

"Turn around!" he ordered as he heard Veronica groan with despair as she understood her fate.

Sam watched as the woman slowly turned her back to the man as she looked back over her shoulder with a plea for mercy, of which there would be none!

"Get on your knees!" Roger commanded and when she did not obey, he kicked her knees from behind making her collapse.

Veronica was crying and she wanted to plead for her life but she knew it was of no use. This was the end. She and Teddy would die in just a few minutes. She had gambled with their lives and lost.

Roger stilled his nerve, as he prepared to execute the woman whom he had at one time loved. However, he knew that he loved himself even more. He aimed the gun at the back of her head as she cried and made incoherent pleas for her life. He felt as if he was going to be sick. His finger was tightening on the trigger and he was anticipating the kick of the pistol in his hand.

Sam was moving even as Roger took aim. Sam's hand swung

up and caught the wrist of the executioner's hand that was holding the gun an inch from the young mother's head. Sam pulled the gun straight up and into the other man's face even as the gun fired a bullet into the air. Sam could hear the bad guy's nose break and then felt the warmth of the other man's blood on his hand as the bad guy screamed in pain.

Sam's knee then slammed into the bad guy's groin and he felt him go limp. The would-be executioner collapsed face down on the ground. Sam then knelt on his back. He grabbed the other man's head by the by the hair and proceeded to slam his face into the ground until he moved no more. Sam was reaching into his overalls to retrieve his knife to finish the job when he heard the woman screaming. He looked up and saw her watching the beating he was giving in total terror. Sam knew that the man he had at his total mercy deserved death but the terrified woman deserved his assistance and comfort even more.

"I'm here to protect you," he said as he let Roger's bloody face fall into the dirt.

Sam realized that he was here to rescue this woman who was terrified and lost, not to perform an execution. He moved off of the now prostrate Roger and helped her to stand. She suddenly hugged him with the desperation of a drowning person grabbing a life preserver.

"He was going to kill me!" she sobbed into Sam's chest.

"I know. We need to get out of here now," he said as calmly as he could but was unsure just how long they truly had before more bad guys might arrive.

She looked up at him and then nodded that she understood. Sam bent down and picked up Roger's gun which he tossed into the brush before he guided Veronica back towards her car. It was a quick walk back up the trail and they could see that Teddy was still slumped over in the front seat. Veronica broke away from Sam and ran to the passenger side of the car. She opened the door and started hugging and kissing her son who was just beginning to recover from his drugging.

Sam watched reunion of the mother to her comatose son and

began to consider all that he had heard during the woman's interrogation. He knew that the bad guy had tracked her from a long distance. There was no doubt in his mind that there were tracking devices in their things and likely on the car itself. He would need to deal with those quickly or there was no hope for their escape. He also knew there were things they had to take with them. To do that the easiest way was to move the BMW to where his Bronco was parked. He opened the driver's door and slipped behind the wheel and saw that the keys were still in the ignition.

"Get in," he said calmly but with authority as he started the BMW.

Veronica quickly moved to the back seat and as soon as her door was closed Sam backed the car onto the paved road and then drove it into the school parking lot and parked next to his Bronco.

"Get what you need and put it in the back of my car," he said as he got out and went to the passenger side where he quickly pulled Teddy out and put him into the back seat of the Bronco.

Veronica grabbed the gym bag and her purse and put them into the other man's car. She opened the back of the BMW and grabbed both her and Teddy's bags. Her rescuer took her bag from her and effortlessly put it into the back of his Bronco. She then started to get Teddy's tablet but her rescuer took it from her and put it back into the BMW.

"Any other electronics that you have on you? Cell phones, computers, watches?" he asked quietly.

"Just my computer," she said.

"Are the records you took from Percy Brigston on it?" he asked calmly.

"No, they are on a thumb drive," she replied.

"Good, leave the computer here," he said.

Veronica pulled the laptop out of her bag and then left it in the BMW with the tablet.

"Get in! We have to get the hell out of Dodge," he said as he reached back into the BMW and pulled out the keys and in one quick move tossed the keys into the woods across the road.

In his mind he was already calculating just how long he had before the bad guys would start to chase them. If the man in the woods had to walk back to his car back at the fast-food joint, he would have at least an hour. Then he decided he better reduce that safe time by half.

"I should have taken his cell phone as well. If he has friends nearby, he will be back in business pretty damn quick. Too late for that now," he thought as he got behind the wheel of his Bronco and sped away.

CHAPTER 12 • A NEW FRIEND

Veronica had joined Teddy in the back seat of the old Bronco and cradled him in her lap as the man who had just rescued them sped away from the place that Roger had picked to kill them. For the first time she looked at her rescuer carefully. His hair was going grey and he had a long and bushy beard. He wore a black cowboy hat, overalls, a long-sleeve tee shirt and work boots. He looked like a true mountain man but was otherwise unremarkable except for one thing, his eyes.

They were the deepest blue she had ever seen but there was more to them than that. Within them there seemed to be confidence and knowledge but with a great deal of sadness or regret. Most of all they made her feel safe.

"Who are you?" she asked from the backseat.

"My name is Sam Stone," he replied as if that explained everything.

"Mom," they heard Teddy say as the effects of the tranquilizer wore off and he could once again move his arms and legs.

Veronica was ecstatic that her son was recovering from the drug that Roger had injected him with. She helped him to sit up but she continued to hold him tight.

"Are you feeling better?" Sam asked the boy.

"I feel kind of tingly all over but I think I am going to be alright," Teddy said but then he asked his mom, "What did you take that made Uncle Roger want to hurt us?"

"That is a very good question but before your mom answers it, we need to get away and I need to have a look through everything you have brought along. Roger," Sam started to say more but paused for effect and then finished, "has been tracking you and knew exactly where you were. I suspect that he has planted tracking devices in things that you take with you frequently. We must find them and get rid of them," he said as he found his way onto the interstate.

Veronica saw a sign that indicated they were about to get onto I-40 and that they were headed toward Raleigh. As soon as they came to the first exit Sam pulled off and turned into a busy truck stop. He pulled all the way to the back and shut off the car.

Sam turned and looked at both of them and said, "Give me your purse and then I want both of you to think of what items you take with you just about everywhere you go."

Veronica handed Sam her purse with only the slightest reluctance. She then tried to think of other items that she had on her all the time. Her cell phone was back in Atlanta. Her computer was left in her car. Then she thought of something that had struck her as odd over her years with Roger. Roger bought her a new roller bag every year. He had told her that he had an obsession about luggage and that it always needed to be clean and in the very best condition. He had also insisted that Teddy have a new backpack every year and was always asking if he liked the one he had.

Sam searched her purse and noted the two thumb drives as well as a significant amount of cash, nearly all hundred-dollar bills. There were also two boxes that contained many diamonds that by themselves were worth hundreds of thousands of dollars. The purse was clean but then he pulled out her wallet. He opened it and quickly noticed a small slot under one of the seams. He felt inside and found a small square item and pulled it out.

"What's that?" asked Teddy.

"This is a state-of-the-art tracking device that is driven off of the global positioning satellite network and it can be detected anywhere in the world. I am certain there was one in your mom's car. I am also certain that there were even smaller ones integrated into your tablet and your mother's computer." Sam

71

said as he looked back at Teddy and Veronica.

"I think you need to check my suitcase as well as Teddy's backpack," Veronica said seriously.

Sam got out of the car and walked to the back and opened it. He started with Teddy's backpack and in a few minutes produced yet another device. He then turned his attention to Veronica's bag and quickly found one more.

He also took a quick look at the gym bag that held a fortune in cash and diamonds but found nothing there. He then checked the clothes that both Veronica and Teddy were wearing. He did not find anything but had not really expected to do so.

"Hand me that duct tape on the floor behind my seat," he said to Teddy.

Teddy saw the roll of silver tape and handed it to him.

Sam quickly tore three separate strips off the roll and pressed one device on to each strip.

"What are you going to do with those?" Veronica asked.

"Have you ever heard of a wild goose chase?" he asked but before she could answer, he chuckled and then continued, "These are our geese."

Sam then walked away and into the parking lot for the tractor trailers. He walked behind a rig and quickly ducked down and slapped one of the tracking devices up under its bumper. He then walked several more spaces and repeated the action. Finally, he walked over to a truck that was at the fuel station and he slapped the last device behind the cab of the truck.

He sprinted back to the Bronco and waited until the truck at the pumps moved out of the lot. He smiled as the truck went on to I-40 heading to the east. About ten minutes later another of the trucks with a tracking device left and also went to the east. Sam looked at his watch and determined that their safe time was nearly up when a driver climbed into the last rig. It slowly left the parking lot and this time Sam followed behind it. This truck went to the west. Sam followed until it came to the interchange and the truck went south onto I-85 while he continued west on I-40.

"That should keep them guessing for a few more hours," he chuckled before becoming serious again, "I need to know who you are and why that guy was trying to kill you."

"I'll tell you but not in front of Teddy," Veronica said quietly and then looked in the backseat and could see that Teddy was listening intently to what the two grownups were saying.

Sam continued to drive through Greensboro as he thought about their situation. He had heard the name "Percy Brigston" during this woman's interrogation. If that bastard was involved in this, they were all in a world of hurt. He needed to know everything and he needed to know it now. He also knew that he had to be careful with this woman who had gone through more terror today than most people would know in their lifetimes. If he pushed her too hard, she might break down.

"So, what is Teddy's mom name?" he asked gently.

"I'm Veronica Tillman," she answered calmly.

"It is nice to meet you Veronica and you as well, Teddy," Sam said cordially, "I'm Sam Stone as I said before. I think you both are very brave and I want you to know that I'm here to help you."

"Why?" asked Teddy.

Sam realized that was going to be a tough question to answer. After all he had been directed to them by a ghost. If he started to tell them that, they would likely be trying to run away from the crazy man with the beard. Still, he needed to say something.

"A friend of mine saw what was happening and he asked me to protect you," he said and hoped that the almost truth would satisfy mother and son.

"Why didn't your friend come along? I mean two of you would have been better than one," Veronica asked as she now had her curiosity aroused as well.

"My friend is disabled. He is good at watching people and seeing when there is something amiss," he replied and thought that being dead was kind of a big disability.

"Where's your friend now?" Teddy asked.

"He's around but he needed to go home," Sam replied and hoped it was enough to satisfy the boy.

"Where are we going now?" Teddy asked and Sam was relieved at the change of subject.

"I think I will take you to my place. We should be safe there but I wish I knew more about how you got to this point and what we are up against," Sam replied and hoped that Veronica would open up a little.

Veronica was deep in her own thoughts. Everything had gone so terribly wrong since she had fled Atlanta. She no longer trusted her own judgement and was terrified that she was going to get Teddy and herself killed.

"Can I trust this stranger?" she asked herself as she looked again at the man named Sam Stone.

Veronica looked out the window as she saw a sign for the exit to the Piedmont Triad International Airport go by.

"How do you know that we will be safe at your place?" she asked.

"Truthfully, I don't know for sure. Right now I don't know how many bad people are after you and what resources they are likely to have," Sam replied in a concerned voice.

"Is there a place we can stop and talk while Teddy stays in the car?" she asked as she looked carefully at him to discern if she could truly trust him.

"I know there are things that you probably would like to spare your son from hearing about but we are being hunted and I believe we may only have at best an hour head start. Stopping to talk just takes away from our head start. I need to make decisions quickly and I really need to know what we may be up against," he said as calmly as possible and he could see Veronica hesitate so he added, "Besides you owe it to your son to tell him why his world has been turned upside down."

Veronica felt her eyes grow moist and she knew that Sam had just told her the truth. Teddy needed to know why all of this was happening. The time of sheltering him was over.

"What do you need to know?" she asked.

"Who was the guy that was trying to kill you back in the woods. I think you said his name was Roger and even Teddy seemed to know who he is," Sam asked.

"He is Roger Culpepper. He was my boss back in Atlanta," Veronica began and decided she had better tell him everything, "I was also his mistress," she finished as she blushed and hoped that Teddy would have no idea what a mistress was.

"He said that he was Teddy's father. Is that true?" Sam asked gently even though he already knew the answer.

"Why do you need to know that?" she replied as glanced back at Teddy who was clearly listening to every word.

"I think he may have been working alone to track you down and get what you took back. If Percy Brigston knew that you had information that could destroy him there would have been a professional hit squad there to take you out. Roger was good today but he had no one watching his back or covering his tracks. He must have had a reason to go lone wolf," Sam replied as he looked at her and added, "I need to know what is motivating Roger."

"I'm sorry Teddy, but it is true. You are Roger Culpepper's son," she said as she looked back at her son who sat there thinking about what he had just heard.

"What is Culpepper's relationship to Brigston?" Sam asked as he followed traffic to the left to avoid going through Winston-Salem on US 421.

"I knew that he managed his investments but just over a day ago I found out that he keeps all the records on Brigston's criminal organization and I think he handles special problems for him as well," Veronica said and hoped that she did not have to be more specific than that on the nature of the criminal organization.

"What kind of special problems?" Sam asked.

"I think he may have killed a Charlotte detective by the name of Jeffrey Williams. I saw his personnel file open on Roger's computer and he had typed the word 'terminated' on his status line. Last night the detective died of a heart attack," Veronica answered.

"You went to Charlotte to meet with this detective?" Sam

asked.

"Yes, I had to find someone who could take the records that I copied to stop what they are doing!" she said and regretted that she had alluded again to the nature of Brigston's Organization so she quickly continued on hoping to move past discussing human trafficking and prostitution in front of her son. "I hoped that I could get his help by warning him that he was about to be killed."

"I see. The records you took are on one of the thumb drives in your purse, correct?" he asked and Veronica nodded that they were.

"What's on the other one?" Sam asked as he glanced at Teddy in the rearview mirror.

Veronica was near panic as she tried to think of how to answer this question without exposing her young son to the depravity of Percy Brigston.

"I don't want to say what I saw but I think Roger recorded a video without Brigston's knowledge. I think he was keeping it in case he needed a way out." Veronica said as she again shuddered at the depravity she had witnessed in that video.

"I think it is safe to say that Percy Brigston does not know of the existence of that recording. If he did, Roger would already be dead," Sam said.

Sam began to analyze what he now knew. Roger Culpepper was a man with a big problem. He had a blackmail video that must be horrific and would destroy Percy Brigston should it ever be made public. If Brigston ever discovered that the video even existed, Roger Culpepper was a dead man. It was fortunate for Veronica and her son that Roger had made that recording. Otherwise, if Veronica had simply copied the records and had been discovered by Roger, he would have used every resource at his disposal to track her down and kill her. This meant that at least to this point there was only one man pursuing them. That would not last much longer because Brigston will grow suspicious of what Roger was up to. The only thing Roger could do next was to create a cover story of a problem with Veronica and that she had taken information and money. Roger will plead that he tried to fix the problem on his own for the benefit of his son.

"We will be safe at my place for a while so we will be going there," Sam said as they neared the west side of Winston-Salem.

"We might only have one person on our tail but soon Brigston will know that something is wrong. Time to start being careful. I'd better take the back way home," Sam said as he exited I-40 and continued west on US 421.

CHAPTER 13 • ROGER'S DESPAIR

Roger Culpepper regained consciousness to the feeling of pain that started between his eyes and then radiated throughout his body. He was face down in the weeds. He slowly tried to push himself up. He felt extremely disoriented as he looked around while he was on his hands and knees waiting to get the strength to rise to his feet. He was trying to figure out where he was and why he was on the ground. It was then he could taste the blood running down his upper lip.

As he stood up, he doubled over with pain emanating from his gonads. He wondered if he had been kicked by a mule but then there was a flash of memory that came into his mind. Veronica was on her knees and he was aiming a gun at the back of her head. He was expecting the kick of the pistol when instead the gun had smashed into his face and then the agony of a knee crushing his balls. He had collapsed to the ground and was pinned there when someone knelt on his back and began to pound his face into the ground until his world went black.

Slowly his memory returned and he recalled why he had to kill Veronica. Someone had stopped him but who and why? He looked around for his gun but it was nowhere to be found. He began to walk back to where they had left Teddy in the BMW but when he got there the car was gone.

"Good! That will make finding her all the easier," he mumbled to himself as he walked towards the road.

As he exited the woods he looked up and there across the road in the school parking lot was Veronica's car.

"Shit," he said as he walked towards the car.

When he got there, he saw that no one was in it. He looked inside and could see that there was a lap top and Teddy's tablet but the keys were gone.

"I have to get back to my car," he said to himself and then realized that his phone was still in his pocket as was his wallet.

It took a few minutes to figure out where he was at and then he called for a car service to come and pick him up.

While he waited for the car to come and pick him up, he tried to think of what to do. The first thing was already started. He needed to get back to his car. He would then get the tracking receiver and he would be able to see where they were. Then he could start the chase again.

"Don't get too far ahead of yourself, Roger," he said to himself. He knew there was now another complication.

There was one big unknown. Who was the person that had stopped him from killing Veronica? He replayed what had happened in the woods over and over in his mind, trying to remember anything he could of the person who had so efficiently subdued him. There was nothing. No sound of anyone approaching. Whoever had intervened had to be a trained professional. The way they had moved and quietly disarmed and subdued him must have come from extensive training in hand-to-hand combat.

"Who would send such a person after Veronica and how could they have even known where to find her?" he wondered to himself as his head throbbed and he continued to feel dizzy.

Roger stood there in the parking lot and was mystified by what had happened. If the person had just been a "Good Samaritan" then why would they have not called the police? If the person had been a cop, then why am I not in custody? If the person had been sent by Brigston, why am I still alive?

Then it hit him. Veronica must have lied about what had happened in Charlotte. She must have contacted somebody who was sending her protection and to get her to a safe house. That stop at the burger joint must have been their rendezvous spot. He must have nabbed Veronica and Teddy just as the first of her rescue team showed up.

"Why did they not just kill me?" he wondered.

Perhaps the person had only been the lead of the team and had no backup. Maybe that person was in a hurry to get Veronica and her information safely away. If it were some legitimate law enforcement agency, they would not have waited to pick Veronica up.

"Why wait for her to drive to Greensboro?" he wondered out loud and then answered his own question. "Because they are Percy's political enemies!"

Percy was first and foremost a political animal. He used blackmail to go after the truly powerful not just here in the United States but around the world. There were many powerful people who would love to have Percy Brigston either eliminated or even better, under their control. Roger thought through the list of who might have wanted Veronica and what she had in her possession. That made much more sense to Roger.

"The blackmailer becomes the blackmailed!" he thought. "That has to be it!" Roger said with absolute certainty as a car pulled into the parking lot.

A pleasant looking black woman got out and started to open the door for him and then she saw his face and said, "Lord almighty, you are hurt. I have a towel in the back and some ice."

The woman opened his door and he slid into the back seat. A moment later she opened the door again and handed him a towel with ice in it. She then quickly got behind the wheel and started the engine.

She looked into the back and asked, "Which hospital do you want me to take you to?"

"No hospital, just get me to that burger joint up on Holden," Roger said as he held the ice on his throbbing nose.

"If I was you, I'd get to a hospital. You got yourself a broken nose for sure and it will need to be put back in place," she said.

"Just take me where I said and I will see to my own nose," he said with irritation.

The woman just shrugged and started up the road the way

he had come earlier. The blood dripping from his nose slowed and the ice did numb the pain. The drive back seemed so much shorter and before he knew it, they pulled into the parking lot. He had paid for the ride with the credit card associated with his phone but he did feel that a gratuity was in order. He found a fifty in his wallet and handed to her and then he offered the bloody towel back to her.

"You just go ahead and keep that," the driver said just before she drove away.

Roger walked over to his car and got in. He quickly found the tracking receiver and turned it on. In just a couple of minutes he had all three of the remaining tracking chips identified but something was odd. They were not moving in unison. The two that should be with Veronica were moving east on I-40 and were nearing Durham. The one that was in Teddy's backpack was moving south on I-85 towards Charlotte.

"Could they have split up? Why?" he wondered as he watched the monitor.

Then he noticed that even the two moving east could not be in a single vehicle. Roger felt sick.

"They must have a whole team and they sent Teddy away for some reason. They must have at least two vehicles traveling east and probably one has Veronica and the other her suitcase," he said as he knew he could no longer continue to work alone.

Roger moaned as he knew that he had to come up with a cover story to convince Percy Brigston of why he had not called him upon the discovery of the theft from his office.

"Think, Roger!" he said in frustration as he continued to watch the tracking receiver.

He knew that he would have to tell Brigston about the theft of the records and of much less importance the cash and the diamonds. He would not have to admit that he had a video taken that he intended to use as blackmail against his boss. So, the big issue was why he had not called Percy immediately.

"Perhaps the truth will work best after all," he said aloud but his hand shook as he picked up his phone.

He hit the button to call Percy Brigston. The phone rang a couple of times and then he heard his boss's voice.

"We have a serious problem," he said as calmly as he could.

"Just what sort of a problem?" asked the British accent on the phone but there was a tone of apprehension.

"Veronica has copied our records from my office and I believe that she is now in the control of one of your enemies," Roger said and cringed as he awaited Brigston's wrath.

There was only stunned silence on the phone. Roger tried to continue by encapsulating what had happened in the last twenty-four hours.

"We need to find out who our adversary is and we need to at least try to catch whoever has Veronica and your son," Percy Brigston said calmly over the phone.

"Yes sir. I will start contacting our resources. Maybe we can get lucky and catch her before they can debrief her," he said with hope.

"Unlikely," was the single word response.

"But we have to try!" Roger said.

"By all means, do try. However, I want you to find out who's team was sent to get her. I must know who our opposition is." Percy said more seriously than Roger had ever heard him before.

"Yes sir!" Roger said and was trying to think how he would accomplish the command.

"We also need to suspend all operations until this is behind us. This will be particularly painful with operation Lorelei. That will be a shame since there were several new big fish coming into our net," Percy Brigston said with regret.

Roger cringed at Brigston's words and knew there were repercussions yet to come.

"And Roger, I hope that in the future you will heed my council that a man should not have emotional attachments and be in any way influenced by such foolishness as love. In this world you are either a master or a slave. You had forgotten this with Veronica!" Percy said as he ended the call.

Roger, for the first time looked into the rearview mirror and could see himself. He looked like he had been in a brawl with a heavy-weight boxer. Both of his eyes were black and his nose was crooked. There was dried blood all the way down to his chin and onto his shirt.

He picked up his phone again and started making calls. It took nearly an hour to contact resources along the interstate going to Raleigh and even as he was making the call the two trackers that had been moving on I-40 split at the interchange for I-85 and I-40. Suddenly one device was headed on towards Raleigh while the other was headed north through Durham. The device for Teddy continued past Charlotte and was now headed back towards Atlanta.

"Chasing those two ghosts is probably a waste of time but we have to try," he mumbled to himself.

It was then that an unmarked police car pulled up next to his and he watched as a man who was in his fifties got out and into Roger's car on the passenger side. The man looked at him and arched his eyebrows at Roger's damaged face.

"Somebody jacked you up pretty good," he said.

"I take it you are Dewy Wilkins?" Roger asked and the man nodded that he was correctly identified.

"I want you to find the person that did this to me," Roger said.

"So, what do you know about the person?" the cop asked.

Roger then recounted how he had been attacked. Wilkins listened with interest as Roger described how he had abducted Veronica and Teddy and had taken them to the Saferight Nature Reserve.

"That's all I know about the person," Roger concluded.

"I'll get some people on it. The best thing we can do right now is start looking at footage from security cameras in the area. I have a couple of people that can collect everything in this area as well as the route you took down to that nature reserve," Wilkins said but then looked at Roger's face again. "You want me to get a doctor to look at that nose? It needs to be set for it to heal right or you're going to be an ugly guy for the rest of your life."

"Do you have someone that can keep this quiet? We don't need any unnecessary attention," Roger said as he felt the throbbing of his broken nose.

"No problem," the cop said and he quickly dialed someone.

"Hi Doc. Yeah, it's me. I got customer for you. Broken nose and maybe some other cuts and scrapes that need to be cleaned up," Wilkins said and then listened. "This needs to be kept really quiet so just you and no one else." He listened again and said, "Ok, he'll be there at five-thirty."

The detective then pulled out a note pad, wrote an address down tore the sheet out, and handed it to Roger. "It will take you about fifteen minutes to get there. You can trust Doc. He owes me on some stuff that needed to be covered up."

Roger's eyebrow arched but decided whatever the crooked cop had on the doctor he did not need to know at the moment. He then looked at the time and saw that he had about twenty minutes to get to the doctor's office.

"I'll let you know what we find out but it might take us a couple of days." Wilkins said as he got out of Roger's car.

Roger put the directions to the doctor into his phone and started to drive away. His phone rang almost as soon as he left the parking lot.

"Yes," he said as he answered the incoming call.

"This is Harris with the Durham County Sheriff's Department. We found the tracking chip you asked us to find. It was attached to the bumper of a tractor trailer going north on I-85. I don't think the driver had any idea that it was there. Do you want us to hold the driver?" Deputy Harris asked.

"No need. Thank you, Harris," Roger said and quickly ended the call.

He had no doubt that the other two trackers were going to be ghosts as well.

"I had to try. I really need a break and I need it fast," he thought but he knew he was unlikely to have his luck change any time soon.

For the first time in his life Roger Culpepper felt he was on the verge of total defeat.

CHAPTER 14 • FLEEING
TO THE MOUNTAINS

Veronica watched as the countryside slipped by. At first they remained on a road that looked just like any other interstate she had ever been on. She could tell by the angle of the sun that they were going west. About a half hour had gone by when they passed under I-77 and she began wonder just where Sam's home was.

"Just how far away is your home?" Veronica asked.

"It is still a couple of hours away. I live in the mountains," Sam replied.

"That kind of fits with the way you dress and look," Veronica said with a slight chuckle. "Have you always lived in the mountains?"

"No, I grew up in the Los Angeles area but that was a long time ago now," he replied.

"Wow, that is quite a change in life styles. Did your work bring you to North Carolina?" she asked, trying to make conversation to pass the time but also to get to know the man to whom she had entrusted the lives of both herself and her son.

"I moved here when I retired. I like to ride motorcycles and this part of the country has always been one of my favorite places to ride," he replied.

"What kind of work did you retire from?" she asked and when he did not answer right away, she wondered if he may not have heard her.

"I was in the military for a while and then I did some contract work for the government," he answered and Veronica could tell that while the answer was truthful it was also uninformative.

She decided to try a different tack to get the man to open up. "Do you have a family?"

It was then that she could see pain on the man's face and she understood that she had inadvertently hit a raw nerve.

Sam had realized that Veronica was trying get some intelligence on just who held her life in his hands. That was fair enough but he had spent the last eight years building walls around the open wounds that had been left by a long and action-packed life. A life that had been filled with secrets that could never be shared and tragedies that had brought him to his knees. Most of those things came from his thirty-year career in Special Forces and as a professional "spook" but not all. The question about family brought back a failure that had been one he had made all by himself. He had tried to blame his failed family on the career he had undertaken but the truth was that he had failed miserably as a father by his own volition.

"I am a widower. My wife passed away a little over ten years ago," he said and his voice broke a little.

Veronica felt physically ill as she realized that she had opened a wound that Sam Stone would have preferred to have been left alone but then he continued on.

"She had pancreatic cancer. It was discovered too late and it was a very aggressive type. She died six months after her diagnosis," Sam replied as he recalled those painful last few days of his wife's life.

"I'm sorry! I did not mean to pry," Veronica said but she knew there was no way for her to ever fully comprehend what this man had gone through.

She was surprised when Sam continued but he felt strangely compelled to tell the rest of his family's story. "We had two daughters. They're around your age," he said and then paused for a few seconds. "I was not a good father. I provided for their material needs. I set high goals for them and held them to them. I gave them discipline to know right from wrong." Again he seemed to have trouble continuing but with a deep sigh he said, "What I did not give them was understanding, encouragement, and most of all, love. After their mother died, they made it clear that they no longer wanted anything to do with me."

Now Veronica wanted to crawl into a hole as she felt the pain that was contained in his words. All she could say was, "I'm so sorry," which felt deeply inadequate.

"Not your fault that any of that happened," he said as he seemed to pull himself back from his melancholy before continuing. "One of the things that I have learned as I have grown older is that a person should never regret any day that they have been given. Good days give you happiness, bad days give you experience, the worst days teach you lessons, and the best days give you memories. I've had an interesting life with plenty of every kind of days," Sam said as a slight smile formed on his face.

Veronica felt her eyes moisten as she saw that this man had accepted the bad things in his life, was willing to learn the lesson that the worst things the world could throw at him, and yet he had his memories and tried to be happy.

Sam exited US 421 as he passed through Wilkesboro onto route 268 and headed west. Again they were quiet for a while and Veronica looked out the window. As the miles flew by they passed a lake that had several picnic areas that looked inviting, then the road became curvier and there was almost no traffic.

"After we get to your house, what do we do then?" Veronica asked and realized she was prepared to follow whatever plan Sam Stone thought was the right thing to do.

Sam was thoughtful. "I think the first thing to do is for me to look at what is on those two thumb drives. We have to figure out what we have on Brigston and whom we can trust because we are going to need some powerful allies. We must take Percy Brigston down or all three of us will be dead. It's that simple."

"You talk like you know him," Veronica said.

Sam knew that question was coming. His mind was filled with images of death and betrayal.

Then he said, "I have never met the man but I know what he is."

The way he said that sent a shiver down Veronica's spine.

"How did you get tied up with this Roger Culpepper?" Sam asked as he wanted to know more about her.

Veronica squirmed. She now had her own memories stirred but she needed to tell him and she knew that Teddy was probably listening as well.

"I grew up very poor down in Atlanta with just my mom. I was planning on going to college to find a way out of the poverty that I had grown up in. I was introduced to Roger when I was looking for a summer job. Roger introduced me to a life of unbelievable wealth and privilege," she began and then felt the shame of what she had become. "I wanted what he could give and he wanted me," she said as her voice quivered.

Sam reached over and gently squeezed her hand to reassure and to tell her that he now knew all that he needed to know. However, Veronica was not finished. She had to tell her son how he had come to be.

"At first it seemed as if we had fallen in love with each other, but he was a married man. I was jealous and I wanted him to leave his wife and marry me. Then I got pregnant," she said as she looked at Teddy who was listening in the back seat, "and I thought that would force him to leave his wife for me but I could not have been more wrong!" she said as she wiped away a tear that ran down her face before she continued. "He told me that I had two choices. The first was for me to stay and be his mistress and raise my son as my illegitimate child. If I did that, he would continue to be my sugar daddy and support us both. On the other hand, if I told anyone that Teddy was his son, then he would have me declared unfit to be a mother and he would take Teddy from me. He said that he would kick me out on the street and I would never see Teddy again. There was no choice. I could never give up my child and I'm ashamed to say it, I did not want to be poor again."

Veronica sobbed softly as she once again realized that she had sold herself to Roger Culpepper. She remembered but would not tell Sam Stone or her son just what being Roger's mistress was truly like. He controlled everything in her life. She was cut off from her mother. She had to spend countless hours in the gym to maintain her youthful appearance and fit body. She was only permitted to wear clothes that he picked out for her. He dictated what hair style she would have. The worst of it was submitting to his deviant sexual fantasies. No, she would never share with anyone the hell she had lived.

Veronica had lived as his personal slave and would have continued to do so in order to provide for Teddy. She lived a life of quiet despair that would never change until Roger Culpepper decided to throw her away like a piece of trash. At least that was true until yesterday when she had learned of just what Roger Culpepper, in the service of Percy Brigston, was really doing. She could no longer tolerate the thought of him touching her. She shivered as she again recalled the look on that young girl's face. It would haunt her forever! She was determined to stop them or she would die trying.

Then she felt Teddy's arms wrap around her from the back seat as he said, "I love you, Mom!"

"I knew I should have killed that bastard," Sam said softly.

Veronica noticed that they were coming to a stop sign and that there was a four-lane highway that they would need to cross. On the other side of the road was a gas station. When Sam had crossed the road, he pulled into the station.

"How about a quick break?" he said as he parked away from the building.

They entered the store and Sam directed them to the restrooms. He and Teddy went into the men's room while Veronica went through the other door.

"Your mom is a good woman, son. Never forget that," he said as they washed their hands.

"I know," young Teddy said as he looked up at him. "Roger was going to kill me, too. When he had me under that drug, I could not move but I heard what he was saying. He's a bad man."

"Yes, he is, but we're going to stop him," Sam said as he tousled the boy's hair.

They stepped back out and waited for Veronica to join them. Sam noticed that Teddy was looking longingly at the sodas.

"I think I could use something to drink. How about you?" Sam asked the boy just as Veronica joined them.

They walked over to the coolers containing various beverages and Teddy quickly pulled out a Coke for himself while Sam reached in and got a bottle of water.

"I guess I'll settle for water too, but after today I could use something a little stronger," Veronica said jokingly as she also selected a bottle of water.

"I think I can arrange that for you," Sam said with a chuckle as Veronica wondered what he meant by that.

They walked to the cashier and Veronica watched as Sam reached into his overalls and pulled out a large roll of money. He sat a twenty on the counter and waited for his change. They walked back out to the Bronco and climbed in. Teddy was happily gulping his drink down as Veronica opened her water and took a sip. Then she watched as Sam reached under his seat and pulled out a pint mason jar and unscrewed the top before handing it to her.

"This is a little stronger than your water, so go ahead and help yourself," he said with a smile.

"What is it?" Veronica asked as she looked at the amber liquid in the jar as her nose inhaled the smell of whiskey.

"That is some of the finest moonshine you will ever taste. It is called Toe River Rye," he said as he pulled back out of the station and started down what was just a country road.

Veronica lifted the jar to her lips and sipped at the home-made liquor. She had always been a mixed drink kind of person. As the 'shine touched her tongue she became aware of a faintly sweet taste that was followed by a rich oak flavor and then a warm pleasant fire in the back of her mouth. She held the jar as she felt the moonshine warm her stomach and then course through her body. Finally she felt some of the tension in her body release.

"So, what do think of it?" Sam asked as he made yet another turn onto a different road.

Veronica did not answer but instead lifted the jar again and took a bigger sip of the amber liquid. She then put the lid back on the jar and handed it back to Sam.

"Thank you. That is interesting," she said before sipping from her water bottle again.

Sam chuckled again as he put the jar back under his seat and continued to drive on a road that was becoming increasingly twisted.

They drove a while before once again they came to another intersection and this time Sam went to the right. Soon the road was steadily climbing up into a much higher elevation. Veronica could feel the temperature drop as he they sped up the highway.

She lost track of the number of turns that Sam had taken but she had no reason to even try to do so. She had come to fully trust this man who had saved her. Then she saw a tunnel coming up and it had a sign that announced that it was the Little Switzerland Tunnel.

"That's so cool!" Teddy said from the back seat as they were about to enter it.

Just a short distance after the tunnel there was another sign that announced the exit would lead to Little Switzerland. Sam made the left turn to go toward the town and a state route labeled 226A. She noticed that there was a resort as they pulled off but then Sam followed the road that led away from it. They came to a stop sign and she could see the Little Switzerland Café and General Store along with the Post Office just across the street.

Sam quickly maneuvered on to a road called Bear Wallow. Veronica was stunned by the mountain vistas that flashed before her. Then they were once again plunged into the vibrant mountain woods before they passed through a one-lane tunnel. He continued for a few miles before he made a turn to left onto a road that did not have any center lines, which he followed until he came to a gate.

Sam got out of the Bronco and walked over to the gate to open it. Veronica saw that there was a "no trespass" sign posted. She could also see a building just a short distance from the gate. Sam then returned to the car.

He looked at Veronica and said, "This is my home."

CHAPTER 15 • ROGER'S WOUNDS

R oger arrived at the doctor's office that was not far from the hospital. He walked to the front door and tapped on the glass with his knuckle, becoming aware of how much dried blood was on his hands. He also could see his reflection in the glass door. He looked as bad as he felt. Then he saw a tall thin man come to the door wearing a white coat. He looked at Roger and unlocked the door.

"Come on in," the man said as he held the door open.

Roger entered a typical waiting room with its uncomfortable chairs and a table with old magazines on it. There were the typical information brochures in a rack by the check-in window. Everything seemed old and worn.

"Right this way," the doctor said as he opened a door that led to the examination rooms.

They entered a room that had the number one in the door along with a tray that would hold a file after a nurse had done an initial exam.

"Have a seat and let me take a look at you," the doctor said.

Roger sat up on the table while the doctor pointed a light into each of his eyes.

"Follow my finger with just your eyes," the doctor said and Roger did.

"You have a mild concussion," the doctor said and then put his stethoscope onto Roger's back, "Deep breaths," he instructed and Roger complied.

"Take off your shirt," the doctor instructed.

"You're supposed to fix my nose. Why do you need my shirt off?" he asked showing his irritation.

"You got knocked around pretty good. I already know that you have a mild concussion and your nose is broken. I want to make sure you do not have more injuries that could send you to the emergency room if not treated. Wilkins said you wanted this all kept quiet and a trip to an emergency room would not be conducive to your desired outcome. Now take off your shirt and let me do my job," the man in the white coat said with his own impatience.

Roger removed his shirt and the doctor started to poke and prod his back which was much more tender than he had expected.

"There is nothing broken but starting tomorrow you are going to feel pretty tender for the next week or so. Whoever beat the shit out of you must be an expert at that sort of thing. Did he hit you anywhere else?" the doctor asked.

"Yeah, he kicked me in the nuts," Roger answered with embarrassment.

"Drop your pants," the doctor said with a shrug.

Roger complied and felt the indignity of the doctor examining his privates.

"You will be sore for a few days. Put some ice on them to bring the swelling down. Now let me take a care of that nose," the doctor said.

Roger flinched with pain as the doctor probed his nose before saying, "This will hurt a little," as his hands gripped his nose and expertly moved the bones back into alignment.

The pain was severe and there was fresh blood. The doctor then packed his nostrils with gauze.

"Take some over the counter pain relievers and don't blow or pick your nose. You can take the gauze out in a day or so. If it starts to bleed again and you can't stop it give me a call," the doctor said as he handed him a card with his number.

"Do you have a place I could clean up a little?" Roger asked.

"I have a shower in my personal office and I have an extra shirt that should fit you as well," the doctor said as they walked down the hall.

Fifteen minutes later Roger was getting back into his car. He had no idea what he should do next. He drove around and then saw a hotel and decided he'd better check in. Wilkins had said it would be at least a couple of days before he had any news. He walked into the lobby and waited for the clerk to return to the desk. He was growing impatient when an attractive young woman with red hair came out of a back office.

"May I..." she started and then just stood there with her mouth open as her eyes revealed her shock at the look of Roger's beaten face, "...help you?" she managed to finish.

"I need a room for few nights," he said.

"Do you have a reservation?" she asked as her eyes darted at him and then back to her keyboard.

"No, will that be a problem?" he replied.

"No, sir. May I see your driver's license and a credit card?" the clerk asked.

Roger handed her his fake license and the matching credit card. In a few moments she handed him a room key and pointed to his room number on the inside of the key holder.

"Is there an ice machine near the room?" he asked.

"Yes, sir. It's right next to the elevator. Would you like me to get you an extra-large bucket and bring it to your room?" she asked trying to be helpful.

"That would be kind of you," he said before he turned to go park his car.

A few minutes later he carried his few possessions into the hotel, looked at the key holder, and noted that he was in room 312. He found it quickly and had just set his belongings down when there was a knock on the door. He opened it to find the young red-headed clerk there with a large bucket of ice.

She walked in and placed the bucket near the sink. Roger watched her and briefly wondered what it would cost to get her into bed but then his swollen testicles told him that was not such a good idea.

"Is there anything else that I can get for you?" she asked as she flashed a pretty smile.

"As a matter of fact, there is. I had an accident earlier today. I really need some Ibuprofen and some new clothes. Jeans, shirt, underwear and socks. Nothing fancy," he said and then added, "I need toiletries as well."

"I'm not sure if I can do that," she said as she began to look a little leerily at him.

Roger put five one-hundred-dollar bills on the counter and said, "You can keep the change."

The clerk scooped up the money and asked, "What size pants?"

"Let me write it down for you," he said.

Roger grabbed a note pad and pen and wrote down what he needed. Then he let her out the door and regretted that he would not get to find out what her price was.

"All women are whores and you just need to negotiate the price," he said to himself with his sense of superiority.

He then filled two hand towels with ice and applied them to his injuries.

"As for the bastard that did this to me, he will pay dearly and it will take him a long time to die," Roger added with a groan.

CHAPTER 16 • SANCTUARY

Veronica had expected Sam's house to be just beyond the building she had seen near the gate but he drove by that building and put the Bronco into four-wheel-drive as the road began to climb up the side of a mountain. It took over five minutes before they rounded a curve and came upon a house perched on the side of the mountain. There was a separate detached garage tucked off to the side that looked big enough to hold three cars. Sam turned the Bronco so that it was pointed back down the road they had just come up. Then out of the corner of her eye she saw a large black shape charging through the woods.

"Is that a bear?" Veronica asked just before the biggest dog she had ever seen emerged from the woods and ran to the Bronco's driver's door.

"No, that is the dog that lives with me. His name is Diesel," Sam answered as the dog's massive black head came through Sam's window.

Sam opened the door and he and the dog exchanged greetings as only dog and human could. It was as if they had not seen each other for months even though Sam had only left home that morning,

"Come on and let me introduce you to my roommate and I'll show you around my home," Sam said, clearly glad to have company.

Sam found himself excited to have the opportunity to show Veronica and Teddy his home and its many wonders, because he did consider it an enchanted place. It hit him just how odd his excitement was since he had lived here for eight years but this was the first time that anyone other than himself had seen it. Even more amazing was that until he had driven by the lower garage, he had never had any desire to have visitors. This had been his sanctuary but now he understood that Veronica and Teddy also needed it as much as he did.

Veronica opened the door and stepped out and continued to look around at the most astounding place she had ever seen. The view from the parking area was breathtaking and she intuitively knew that from the other side of the house the view would also be spectacular. As she scanned the area, she spotted water crashing down the side of the mountain before it disappeared into the woods below where a deeper roar spoke of an even larger stream.

Sam had gone to the back of the Bronco and was pulling their bags out. Veronica reached back into the car and got her purse and the gym bag with the cash. Teddy was looking around when Diesel walked up and looked him over before he pushed up against the boy and demanded to have his head rubbed, which Teddy did with great pleasure.

Sam carried their bags to the front door, which had never been locked in eight years, and opened it up. Diesel led them into the main living area. Veronica had not known what to expect as she stepped through the door but she found herself in a great-room with a vaulted ceiling that contained a well-appointed kitchen area on one side. Past that there was a stunning living area with every chair positioned to take advantage of the far-off mountain vistas. It struck her with surprise at just how meticulously the house was maintained. It looked as if there were a full-time maid that cleaned daily and, even more shocking for a man who lived alone, there was no clutter. Everything had a place and was in that place. She noticed there were French doors that obviously led off to a large deck. Next she noted that there was a door that led to what she assumed were Sam's sleeping quarters.

Sam took their bags and went through that door with

Veronica and Teddy in tow. There was a king-sized bed that was neatly made and was positioned toward a large window that again embraced the magnificent view.

"You and Teddy will bunk out in here," he said before continuing, "the bathroom is through this door."

Sam opened the door that led into a bathroom which had a massive soaking tub and as she turned to look across the room there was the largest walk-in shower she ever seen. There was yet another door off of the bathroom that was a walk-in closet and laundry-room combination.

"This is your space," Veronica began to protest.

"It is the only place in the house that is going to accommodate two people and I want you both to be comfortable. I have an office with a separate bath on the lower level and I have a daybed down there. Believe me it is quite comfortable," Sam said and his manner indicated he would not take no for an answer.

Sometime during the tour of the living quarters Teddy had slipped away and it was only then that Veronica noticed that he was gone. She was just looking around for him when she heard his excited voice coming from the main room.

"Mom! You have got to see this!" Teddy yelled from the bedroom doorway.

Veronica went to see what her son had discovered. Teddy was standing by the French doors leading out onto the deck.

"There's a waterfall!" Teddy said with glee.

Veronica walked out onto the deck and instantly was greeted by the sound of water crashing down the mountain and into a large deep pool at the bottom that was crystal clear. She stood at the rail with her mouth hanging open at the sheer beauty of the view below the deck.

"Make yourselves at home. I have a couple of chores to get done and then we can have dinner," Sam announced as he joined them on the deck.

"Is there something I can do to help?" Teddy asked to his mother's delight.

Sam studied the boy for a minute and then said, "Sure, I can always use an extra pair of hands."

Sam and Teddy went back out to the parking area as Diesel bounded happily along. Sam opened the garage and Teddy could see there were many tools in the garage as well as an ATV that was configured with a dump bed. Sam walked across the garage and then opened a secret door. There were a dozen cases of quart jars with an amber liquid as well as stacks of empty jars. In the back Teddy noticed the biggest refrigerator he had ever seen, a restaurant-sized unit. Next to it on the floor were three five-gallon plastic buckets.

"We need to change these buckets out," Sam told the boy as he opened the refrigerator to reveal that there was a similar number of buckets on the inside.

Sam picked up one in each of his hands and invited Teddy to pick up the third and pull it out of the refrigerator. Sam could see that Teddy was struggling to lift the weight but he let the boy complete the job on his own. They then picked up the buckets that had been sitting on the floor and put them into the refrigerator.

Teddy felt good to be helping Sam in this simple task. He had never had a man to look up to before. He had no idea why they were doing the bucket exchange but that did not matter.

"Thanks Teddy, you're a big help," Sam said and watched as the boy lit up at the praise, "Now we have to get the supplies out of the back of the Bronco and move them down to what we call the still house. Have you ever driven an ATV?" Sam asked as they walked over to the ATV. Teddy shook his head that he had not.

Sam opened the driver's door and then slid across the seat and into the passenger seat, leaving the driver's seat open. He indicated that Teddy was to get behind the wheel. The boy hesitated for a moment but when Sam patted the driver's seat he quickly complied with a grin. Sam smiled at the boy gripping the steering wheel with wonder on his face.

"The pedal on the right is the gas and the pedal on the left is the brake. The lever here is the gear shift. 'L' is used to go up and down steep trails, 'H' makes you go fast, and 'R' makes you go backwards. 'P' is where you put it when you are not going anywhere. Turn the key to start it," Sam said he sat back and waited for the fun to begin.

Teddy turned the key and the motor started instantly. He then put it in "H" and the ATV leapt out of the garage as Teddy slammed on the brake, throwing both Sam and himself forward. Sam was laughing as he watched the shocked look on the young boy's face.

"Guess I forgot to tell you to put your foot on the brake when you put it into gear," Sam said as he chuckled in a good-natured way that had Teddy laughing as well.

When they had both had a good laugh Sam said, "You're doing fine, son. We all learn from our mistakes. Now, try it again."

Teddy knew that Sam wanted him to learn this. He stepped on the brake and looked into the old man's face as he moved the lever into the 'H' position. He then slowly let his foot off the brake, then lightly pressed the gas and pulled the ATV up next to the Bronco. He then put it in park as Sam jumped out and started to move the heavy bags of grain and sugar into the truck bed. Teddy joined him and Sam slowed down to allow the boy to help move each bag into the back of the ATV.

After loading the last bag of sugar into the bed of the ATV, Sam turned to Teddy and said, "Get behind the wheel."

This time Teddy was much more confident as he got behind the wheel, started the motor, and moved the gear-shift into drive with his foot on the brake. Sam pointed to a trail away from the house. It was not a particularly difficult trail but it did require Teddy to watch what he was doing. Sam would occasionally correct his steering but mostly he allowed Teddy to drive them the quarter of a mile to his still.

Teddy was smiling literally from ear to ear as he maneuvered the ATV down the trail until they came to a shed-size building. It had a large porch area with a comfortable-looking rocking chair. Sam pointed to where he should park the ATV. Sam then got out and opened the door to the small building. Teddy followed Sam in and saw several large blue barrels standing along one wall. Sam walked by these and went to three large storage bins. One was labeled "corn," a second "rye," and the third "sugar." He opened each of these and then walked back out to the ATV. Teddy helped Sam carry each of the heavy sacks into the building and put them in their respective lockers. Sam knew that he could have done the job in half the time alone but he also knew it was important that this boy feel a sense of purpose and accomplishment.

"Thank you for helping, Teddy!" Sam said as they again climbed into the ATV. "Take us home!"

Sam had never known a greater joy than seeing the look on Teddy's face as he drove the ATV back up the trail and into the garage with no further instruction from Sam.

"Great job!" said Sam as they exited the vehicle. "I might have to keep you around for a while. I think I could use something to eat. How about you?" he asked and watched as the boy glowed with a sense of accomplishment that would last for the rest of his life and nodded enthusiastically.

Sam chuckled softly as Teddy sprinted for the house to tell his mom about what he had done. He entered the house and could hear the boy telling his mother how he had driven the ATV. Sam knew he needed to get something fixed for their dinner. He reached into his freezer and pulled out three servings of his Brunswick Stew. He was just starting to warm the stew up when Veronica came back into the house.

"You made his day and maybe his year," Veronica said with a giggle as they could hear Teddy playing with the dog on the deck. "Thank you for letting him drive your ATV. I am not sure I have ever seen him this happy!" Veronica said and Sam could see that the young woman almost sparkled with happiness.

"He's a good boy and he has the makings of a good man. Your job is to help him discover what is inside him," Sam said as he stirred the stew.

"Is there anything I can do to help you?" she asked.

"Over in that breadbox there is a loaf of bread. Go ahead and cut us a few slices," Sam said.

Veronica opened the breadbox and found a large loaf of what appeared to be home-made bread. There was a large serrated knife by the box. She pulled out the loaf and watched as crumbs broke away from the crusty bread as she sliced it. She could already smell the delicious aroma of the bread as the first slice fell away.

"This looks like delicious bread. Does someone bake it locally?" she asked.

"Yeah, me," replied Sam as he tasted the stew and decided it was nearly warm enough.

He then reached into the pantry and retrieved three apples. He quickly sliced the apples and placed them in a bowl and put them on the table.

He took the slices of bread from Veronica and put them in the broiler to toast them. When they were done, he put the bread on the table with butter and homemade blackberry preserves. He divided the stew into three bowls and set them on the table as well. Next, he put food into Diesel's bowl.

"Dinner is ready," he announced with a smile.

Veronica retrieved Teddy from the deck and they all sat at the table. Veronica could smell the stew and her stomach growled in anticipation. She picked up her spoon and started to dip it into her bowl.

But then Sam spoke softly, "I have very few rules but one thing I insist on under my roof is that we thank God for the food we are about to eat."

Veronica set down her spoon and Teddy simply looked confused.

Sam put his hands together and bowed his head. Veronica was startled to see Diesel also closing his eyes and lowering his head just like his master.

"Thank you, God, for this food and for the mercies you have shown us this day. Keep us through the coming night and if it is your will into a new day of your making. Amen," Sam said and then smiled at his two guests.

Diesel then went to his bowl and devoured his food.

Veronica and Teddy consumed the savory stew and Sam grinned before joining them.

"This is wonderful!" Veronica said as the delicious food satisfied her hunger as well as comforted her soul.

Sam tried not to smile too much as he watched his guests eat his stew, which consisted of vegetables grown in his garden as well as squirrels and rabbits that he had hunted on his land.

"Best not tell them about that just yet," he thought to himself.

Sam then put some blackberry preserves on his bread and invited Teddy to do the same. Veronica watched as Teddy took a bite and saw a look of joy spread over his face. She tried her own bite of bread and preserves and could not remember tasting anything so wonderful before.

After dinner they went to the deck and listened to the soothing sound of the waterfall. Sam pulled out a jar of 'shine, poured a generous helping for himself, and then looked at Veronica who nodded that she wanted to join him.

They sipped the delightful liquor and noted that Teddy had drifted off to sleep.

"Thank you for everything you have done for us. You have a truly special place here. I think Teddy will never want to leave," Veronica said and wondered if she would want to leave, herself.

"I think Teddy could use a good night's sleep and so could you," Sam said as he stood up and then effortlessly picked up Teddy and carried him into the bedroom.

Veronica watched and became uncomfortable with a feeling that began to build in her. She had willingly given herself to Roger to escape her poverty. Women had always looked to men to take care of them and it was understood that women would take care of what those men wanted in exchange.

"Is that what Sam Stone wants from me?" she wondered but admitted that if it was, she would submit but then she felt shame at her thoughts.

Sam walked back through the door and got back into his seat while he looked out into the darkness.

"You have a wonderful son. I will never forget the look on his face as he drove that ATV," he chuckled as he sipped his glass of 'shine.

Veronica sat nearby and wondered when Sam would make his demand. Sam proceeded to drain the last of the liquid from his glass. He then turned and looked her over. Veronica cringed at what she might have to do but was prepared to give herself to him.

"You need to get some sleep but before you do I need something from you," he said as his eyes looked into her own as she blushed. "I want those two thumb drives. I will need to start reviewing them tonight," he said as he stood up. "And you need to get to bed."

Veronica felt relief that Sam Stone was not looking to use her for his own base needs but there was also another feeling that came over her and she was shocked that it was regret. She retrieved the two thumb drives and gave them to him.

"Veronica, you may feel at peace here tonight. You are safe," Sam said to her as she went to join Teddy in the bed.

CHAPTER 17 • SAM'S JOURNEY

S am looked at the two thumb drives in his hand and felt revulsion at what he would have to witness. He then walked back into the house and closed the French doors behind him. Diesel found a comfortable spot on the sofa.

"Keep an eye on them," he told the dog and then headed down to the lower level of the house.

The downstairs had a pool table in a room at the base of the stairs that he called the game room. There was another set of French doors that led out onto a smaller deck. Off of the game room was his office. It was not a big room but it had a small desk, a bookshelf with a few treasured books, and a daybed. Another door led to the small bathroom that had a shower stall.

Sam took time to shower and put on a pair of exercise shorts and a tee-shirt to sleep in.

"Have to remember that I now have company in the house. Can't just be running around in my skivvies," he thought with a laugh.

He then poured another glass of 'shine and sat down at his computer. He had an internet connection but he only activated it when he needed to be online. Tonight he would not need it. He opened the computer and booted it up. He then took one of the thumb drives and inserted it in one of the USB ports. By scanning the contents, he knew that it was the one that contained the copied files from Roger Culpepper's hard drive.

He removed the thumb drive and put the other one in. It was a video file and his hand shook as he hit the play button. Sam Stone had seen many things in his long career but he had never seen anything that caused the sense of revulsion that he felt as he watched Percy Brigston delight in the sick perversions recorded in that video with that poor adolescent girl. It was clear that the recording was being done surreptitiously. At the end of the video the girl was tied to a bed and was crying with Percy Brigston standing naked by her with a grin on his face. Sam sat there shocked by what he had witnessed but then was surprised that after the video had faded out that there was just a little more audio.

He heard Percy Brigston say, "Now it's your turn, Roger. I have her all broken in for you."

Sam sat still and felt ill. Then anger began to burn deep in his soul. His mind focused on all the interesting ways that those two bastards could be tortured to death. He closed his eyes and wanted to envision his more inventive ideas but the ghosts came to him instead.

They cried with him at the tragedy that he had just witnessed. He felt them embrace him and comfort him. Sam began to cry even harder as he was held by them.

"Now is not the time for anger," they said. "There are victims to be rescued. There are hostages to be freed. Leave vengeance for another day, for that day will come," the ghosts said over and over.

Slowly, Sam pulled himself together, removed the disgusting thumb drive, and inserted the other. The amount of data was massive but it was also well organized. He noticed the personnel files as well as files marked "Financial," "Operations," "Inventory," "Clients," and finally, "Other Assets."

He opened the financial file first and it was what he had expected. It was an accounting of the funds they received and spent as well as where the money was located. A prosecutor would have a field day with the evidence contained in the file. There was also a tremendous amount of documentation on how the massive amounts of funds were laundered at Culpepper's direction. And then a trail of how dirty money was used to pay off various vendors. Clearly, Culpepper Wealth Management was a very busy entity.

Sam opened the operations file next and it documented how the illicit movement of humans was accomplished. There were also reports of operations that had to be closed down for a variety of reasons but one that he found curious was a file marked "Public Relations." He opened that file and began to read how Brigston's Organization occasionally allowed an investigative news team or law enforcement agency to expose a link in their operations. The point of the drill was to show that the existing countermeasures to human trafficking were effective, while in reality they were only a drop in the deep profitmaking bucket.

He opened the inventory and cringed as he saw the number of people being moved around the world. What was most shocking was that they were not all young females. There were boys as well as girls and there were also adults. Brigston apparently wanted to serve the criminal sex trade for every illicit fetish in the marketplace.

The clients file would be a blackmailer's dream. It was divided into categories of buyers: "High End," "Middle," and "Low End." He was the most curious about the "High End" clients but clicked on "Low" first. These were what he expected, the lowlife scum who stocked brothels for the sex trade around the world. He then went to the "High End" and sat there with his mouth open as the names were among the most powerful, wealthy, and famous people in the world.

Sam clicked on some sort of a profile sheet and found the list of the clients with what they currently owned and the location of where their property was being kept. He had been wondering how some of these very public people could get away with having a sex slave. Now he understood that The Organization had sites where the rich and famous could house their human chattel until they wished to use them again. Sam blanched at the thought of the barbaric practice of slavery that was alive and well in the twenty-first century.

The "Middle" buyers were a mixture of fairly well-off people

A SONGBIRD IN FLIGHT

and seemed often to be a place where property of "High End" clients could be resold when they no longer fit their original owners' perverted desires. Most of these clients were outside of the United States.

Sam was growing tired as the enormity of the criminal enterprise he was looking at numbed him. It was difficult for him to grasp just how big The Organization of Percy Brigston was. He had one last file to open and he expected it to be a miscellaneous file where this and that which did not fit elsewhere were kept. That was not the case.

What he found were lists of people that Percy Brigston controlled not by money but by blackmail. It was organized by country, so Sam clicked on the United States. His jaw hit the floor when he saw the number of names. He noticed that he could sort by their current position. He recognized one name as the leading anchor on one of the cable news networks. He clicked on it and there was a summary of what they had on the reporter. In this case there was a recording kept by Brigston in which the anchor was recorded colluding with a political party chairman to play a dirty trick on a candidate that was not of the chairman's choosing. No doubt the recording had the power to end the anchor's career and the anchor would do whatever he was told to keep that recording from seeing the light of day. It was easy to see how Percy Brigston maintained his power if that were true of all the names on the list. Sam noted that while the file documented what was being held over the victims' head, there was no actual evidence in the file.

"I wonder where *that* information is kept!" he thought.

Sam scrolled through the mind-numbing list of names but then came on one that he knew only too well, Art Stanton. Stanton had been Sam's commanding officer on his last operation. Sam opened that file and saw that Stanton had been involved in a fraud that had diverted funds from weapons programs into his and several other influential people's bank accounts. There was no doubt that Stanton would have gone to jail if this were discovered.

109

"Son of a bitch!" Sam said aloud. "That was why that whole mission was arranged! It was also why my team was killed!"

Sam's mind automatically went into flashback mode. His small team was to be covertly inserted into a SouthEast Asian country to neutralize a rogue army officer. The story given to his team was that the officer was getting money by kidnapping teenage girls and selling them into prostitution. He was then using those funds to finance terrorists that wanted to commit another 911-style attack on America. Sam Stone team's objective was to eliminate this threat.

The plan was for him to lead two sniper teams to stalk the target and when he was sure that they had the correct person, to kill him. It was a simple enough mission and one that he and his own team had executed many times before.

He and his teams did a high altitude jump and landed without anyone's notice. He directed the two teams to set up at opposite sides of the enemy's camp with the best views of the compound and to begin their observation duties. He moved to a separate observation point. It was the next morning that things started to no longer make sense.

He was watching when a small worn-out van made its way into the compound. A diminutive local man and an even smaller woman that was presumably his wife got out of the vehicle. It was then that a man dressed in immaculately pressed army fatigues with fancy shoulder boards stepped out of a building and greeted the two civilians. This was not a greeting that one would expect between the local warlord and some peasants. If anything, the officer appeared to be trying to comfort the couple.

Then the officer walked the couple over to a large building. Just as they approached, a small adolescent girl ran from the building and into the embrace of the peasant couple. They were all crying and Sam watched as the officer wiped away his own tears and began giving orders to his men. Soon two soldiers carrying ten-liter petrol cans went to the van and refilled its gas tank.

His field communications link activated.

"Hey, Cap, did you get a load of what just happened?" Higgins said over the secured communications link.

"Yes, I want everyone to stand down on this until we get some more intel," Sam said quietly and tried not to betray his own growing suspicion of the mission.

As the van with the loving family departed, he saw a military truck approaching the camp. Again, the officer came out to greet the truck. After coming to a stop, two men were none too gently ejected from the back of the truck onto the ground. Their hands were tied behind their backs. Several guards converged on the downed men and leveled their weapons at them. Then more troops came and assisted seven young girls to get down from the truck. The oldest of the girls broke free from them and started to kick the prisoners until the officer came and gently restrained and comforted her.

"That tears it! Somebody has screwed the pooch on this one!" Sam said to himself as he watched as the camp doctor appeared to triage the girls before directing them to the camp infirmary.

He watched as the two prisoners were frog-marched to what was obviously a bank of holding cells. It was clear their guards would have liked to have saved the walk but the officer managed to maintain discipline.

His communications link again chirped and Higgins came on. "Are we sure we got the right bad guy?"

"Everybody, stay calm. I'm going to call HQ," he said in a quiet but commanding voice. He switched over to a scrambled voice link.

"Come in Saturn. This is Luna," he said into his microphone and waited and then repeated.

Then in his ears he heard the reply, "Come in Luna. This is Saturn."

"Saturn, we have been observing the target and we do not believe that the intel on the target is correct." Sam said.

"Sam, this Art," said a different voice that came on the line.

"What the hell is going on Art? The guy we have been sent to terminate appears to be the rescuer," Sam said with irritation in his voice.

"Calm down Sam. See if you and your team can get closer to confirm your observations," Sam's commanding officer ordered.

"No need for that! This guy is not a kidnapper!" Sam said with anger.

"Listen Sam, I have seen the file on this guy. He is dirty. I have listened to tapes of him planning attacks on American targets," Art said and then added, "Get close and confirm your observations or kill that bastard!"

"Acknowledged, Luna out," Sam said as he signed off but wanted to puke.

Sam switched back to the local communication link and said, "All team. All team. Close on encampment. HQ has ordered us to gather more intel. Stay out of sight but get close."

His team closed to within a few meters of the camp perimeter, where they could use their listening gear to eavesdrop on conversations of people in the camp. A couple of the men on the team could speak the local language.

Sam's communication link chirped and Higgins's voice came on, "Cap, we are being painted!"

"Why would we be targeted?" Sam wondered but then his world went black as a cruise missel slammed into the center of the installation.

When Sam regained consciousness, he was in the middle of a slaughterhouse. There were bodies and parts of bodies all around him. Then he heard the screams of the wounded, most of whom were simply waiting to die. He could feel blood running down his arm and he looked to see a piece of wood imbedded in his left arm. He quickly began to inventory his injuries. His ears were ringing but he was not totally deaf. He was dizzy and likely suffering from a concussion. There was more blood on his cheek from a small cut.

Slowly he stood up and looked around again. He started to walk through the camp. He stopped at the infirmary and blinked at the mounds of bloody pulp that had been the recently-freed girls and likely the camp doctor. He continued toward what had been the main building, which had virtually ceased to exist and was obviously the target of the missile. Then he heard a cry for help coming from the holding cells.

He walked to the wreckage of the jail and followed the sound of the pleas. Under a collapsed wall he saw a hand move. He studied the sleeve of the uniform and knew that it was the officer that he and his team had been sent here to kill. He started to move debris and soon could see the officer's face. There was no doubt in Sam's mind that the man's wounds were fatal. The man's eyes opened and he looked up at Sam.

"Why?" the officer groaned in English.

Sam could only shrug that he did not know why as he sat down by the dying man.

"You were rescuing the girls that had been kidnapped in the area?" Sam asked.

"Yes, many bad men here. Much money paid to them for girls. My daughter was taken," he said as he coughed blood.

"Are the kidnappers controlled by terrorists?" Sam asked.

"No! Americans!" the officer said and then exhaled his last breath.

Sam slowly stood up and walked toward the perimeter of the camp, looking for his team. He identified two bodies as the remains of one of his sniper teams. He was looking for the other team and was just about to give up when he heard a moan coming from a ditch. He walked toward the sound and found a headless body wearing the uniform of his team. Further along in the the ditch he found Higgins, who moaned again.

Sam jumped into the ditch and quickly began to assess his only fellow survivor. Something had passed through the man's helmet and was buried in his head. Sam found his medical kit and put disinfectant in the wound before gently wrapping the wound with a bandage. Sam then hit the button on his communication link requesting an emergency medical evacuation.

"No resource available. Sorry, Sam," Art's voice said before all communications ceased.

"Why?" moaned Higgins as he looked into Sam's eyes.

Sam felt helpless to answer the question as to why his team was being abandoned after being ordered into the blast zone of a cruise missile that had to have come from an American source. Sam knew that this was the end. He was stuck in a foreign country that had just been attacked. He hoped that he would be executed on the spot. There were so many other less pleasant ways to die...or live.

Then he heard a helicopter and looked up to see a Blackhawk hovering over him. Two men dressed similarly to himself were suddenly in the ditch with him and Higgins.

"Can you walk?" an American asked him and he nodded that he could.

The two Americans made a stretcher out of a poncho and his teams' destroyed weapons. They carried Higgins to the waiting helicopter as Sam stumbled behind them. Once the helicopter was in flight he sat with Higgins and held his hand, feeling his pulse one beat after the next. Then he could not and he knew that Higgins was dead. Sam cried again.

When the helicopter landed Sam was rushed to the ship's surgery. After his wounds had been treated a familiar face entered the cabin he was being kept in.

"Just what the hell were you and your team doing in my team's target area?" asked John Walters, a team leader just like Sam although nearly twenty-five years his junior.

"Art ordered us to do a close-up intel recon. Who ordered the missile?" Sam replied.

"Came from high up. I was told it was a cabinet-level authorization. We had no idea you and your team were in the area until we picked up your emergency med-evac beacon," John said.

"John, can you keep a secret?" Sam asked and John nodded that he could.

Sam spent the next thirty minutes giving a detailed account of what was obviously an ordered assassination of a friendly foreign national and his team's exposure to a missile attack that was clearly intended to kill them.

"My conclusion is that Art Stanton covered a screw-up by hanging your team in the wind," John said, with sadness in his voice. "When he finds out you're still alive he will plead that it was all the 'fog of war' and will beg your forgiveness. I would also say that if you do not accept his apology and let this go, you will be offered an early retirement." This prediction came true in spades over the next several months.

CHAPTER 18 • COMMITTED
TO THE FIGHT

Veronica woke up the next morning in the large comfortable bed she had shared with Teddy. She sat up, leaned back onto the headboard, and once again admired the mountain vista that was there to greet her through the large picture window before her. Teddy was still asleep. It was then that she heard Sam moving in the main room. She slipped out of bed and walked through the door to find him in the kitchen sipping coffee.

"Good morning, Sam" she said as she walked into the room.

Sam looked up at her and smiled. "Good morning! I hope you slept well."

"I had no idea that I was so tired last night. I don't even remember closing my eyes," she replied. She smelled food cooking and, even more enticing, the aroma of the coffee "That coffee smells so good!" she hinted.

Sam poured her a mug, then looked at her and said, "I generally drink my coffee black but I do have some sugar on the table and there is some canned milk in the pantry."

"I'd like both," she replied as she retrieved a spoon for the coffee.

Sam pushed the container of sugar to her before retrieving the can of condensed milk from his large pantry. He set the can on the countertop, reached inside his pocket, and pulled out what Veronica thought at first was a simple pocket knife. Then she heard a click followed by a harder metallic sound as the stiletto knife popped out of the front of the handle, revealing its full four-inch blade. Sam quickly punched two holes into the top of the can before he slid the knife back into its handle and returned it to his pocket.

"That's quite the toy you have there," she said as she added milk to her coffee.

"A man needs a good knife for a lot of purposes, such as opening things," he said, once again looking at her as if he were trying to make a decision.

They sipped their coffee for a few minutes when a timer went off. Sam went to the oven and pulled out a sausage-and-egg casserole. He sat the glass baking pan on a trivet on the table. Veronica felt her hunger grow as the aroma the of the eggs, sausage, and cheese filled the room.

"Is there something I can do to help?" she asked.

"You can set the table," Sam said as he went to slice more of the bread they had eaten the night before.

Veronica was just finishing putting everything in its place when Sam sat down and looked up at her. "I watched the video last night," he said in a haunting voice. Veronica could see the disgust in Sam's blue eyes.

"Did you watch the whole video?" he asked gently.

"No, it was too horrible! That poor girl's screams will haunt me forever," she said as her eyes filled with tears.

"Well, I did," Sam said as he looked off through the windows at the mountains beyond before saying, "Roger was the one who took the video and he also raped that poor child."

"They have to be stopped!" Veronica said as she gripped Sam's hand.

"Yes, they do need to be stopped but it will be dangerous and that is what we need to talk about," Sam said as he held her hand in his calloused own.

"Sam, I know that if they find me they will kill me and Teddy as well. We have nothing to lose," she said with absolute certainty. "That's why it's up to us fight them!"

Sam looked at her for a long moment and then said, "There's

another way out for you and Teddy that should work but it will leave Percy Brigston in place," he said but then paused as he studied her bewildered face. "Old Percy has no idea that he has been betrayed by his closest associate. He would be most interested in knowing that Roger made that video and that he intended to use it at some point to betray him. I could contact Brigston and negotiate a deal that gave him the video back as well as the other information that you took and in exchange, he would let you and Teddy go. You must understand that Brigston is all about knowing other people's secrets while keeping his own indiscretions quiet. Of course, I would insist that you get to keep that money and the diamonds you took if you want to make a deal."

Veronica was shocked that this man that she had thought of as her hero was suggesting a deal with the Devil himself!

Veronica snatched her hand away from his as if it were a snake before she said, "If I wanted to sell my soul to the Devil, I could have just stayed with that demon in Atlanta!" she felt so angry and could not believe that Sam Stone would give up so quickly. "I think Teddy and I should leave here now," she added as she stood up to go back to the bedroom.

"Sit down, Veronica," he said in a firm voice that radiated command.

To her own surprise, Veronica did sit back down in the chair she had just jumped up from.

"I was testing you to see if you truly are committed to seeing this through," he said in a gentle tone. "There will be no one that we can really trust so we will be on our own. That means we will be in danger every minute of every day. I'm certain that by now Brigston is well aware that his security has been compromised and right now he is trying to find out who has the information stolen from Culpepper's office. I doubt that Roger has shared that his blackmail video exists and has also been taken. Right now, they both are trying to figure out just who came to your rescue. Brigston has many enemies that he controls by threat of exposing their own dirty secrets. He is now expecting one of them to call and tell him that he is now under their power. Our enemy is confused for the moment but that will change quickly when no such call comes in." He paused again before he concluded, "What this means is that we have a small amount of time to prepare. Have you ever used a gun?"

Veronica shook her head that she had not.

"That will change today. I will have to show Teddy as well," he said.

"But he just a little boy!" Veronica said with alarm at the thought of her son, just short of his twelfth birthday, learning to use a gun.

"Yes, he is a boy but a boy that one of the most powerful men in the world has sentenced to death. He deserves every chance to live and that includes killing any bastard that comes after him," Sam said coldly.

Veronica sat with her mouth open, trying to process the cold-blooded nature of Sam's reply.

"He's right, Mom," Teddy's voice said from the bedroom doorway.

Veronica turned her head and saw her boy approach the table and then take a seat.

"It's too dangerous! There must be another way!" Veronica said in a panic.

"Mom, they will kill you and me both whether we fight back or not. I don't want to be helpless again like yesterday when Roger tried to kill you while all I could do was wait to be next," Teddy said with absolute certainty.

Veronica looked at Teddy, who still looked like just a normal boy but she knew that yesterday had changed him. He was growing up fast and probably too fast but there was no choice for him. It was not his doing but it is what fate had decreed.

Sam watched as mother and son looked at each other and he knew that Veronica was being confronted by a fundamental change in her relationship with her son. It was the first stirring of independence as a little boy began to change into a man.

"Just in time for breakfast. I'm afraid that I only have coffee, water, or apple cider to drink," Sam said as the boy joined them.

"Cider will be fine," Teddy said as he sat down and licked his lips at the casserole on the table but then he looked at his mother and said, "I will help when they come again. I know they will be coming."

Sam placed a tall glass of cider in front of him and nodded his agreement. He then served them each a generous helping of the casserole. Diesel came and sat near the table as Sam returned to his chair.

He looked at the others and then reached out and took each of their hands and said, "Dear Father in Heaven, we thank you for this food that you have provided. We ask that you would watch over us and bless our labors this day, Amen."

During the prayer, Teddy reached for his mother's hand and held it as he lowered his head and closed his eyes. Teddy did not know much about God but he did know that he trusted in Sam Stone and if Sam Stone trusted God then there must be something to it.

They quickly devoured the food on their plates. Veronica again looked at her son who amazingly seemed so much older this morning than he had just the day before. That terrified her.

"May I have more, please?" Teddy asked and Sam put another large helping on his plate.

"Eat up, we have a lot of chores this morning. Today we will need to go to town to buy some extra supplies and I suspect the two of you might need a few more things as well," Sam said. "When we come back we will begin your basic gun training."

"What kind of chores, Sam?" Teddy asked with interest as he remembered the prior day's adventure on the ATV.

"First we need to clean up the house. I'm afraid my time in the army made me a bit of a neat freak," he said with a chuckle.

"That sounds like a responsibility that I can handle," Veronica said as she realized that she had not really contributed anything since they had arrived.

"Thank you, Veronica. Then Teddy and I will take care of the chickens and the pigs. Ever slopped a hog before?" Sam said with a grin as he looked at the boy who shook his head that he had never done that.

Sam then took his dirty dishes to the sink and proceeded to scrape the plate clean. Teddy watched what he had done and quickly imitated the man he now wanted to be like. Veronica was so proud that Teddy was learning from Sam and hoped that his influence would matter more than Roger's genetic contribution.

CHAPTER 19 • CURSED TIMES

Veronica watched as Teddy and Sam walked out the door. She started by hand-washing the dishes and placing them into an old-style dish drainer. She had grown up without a dishwasher and had sworn that she would never live without one again but here at Sam's place on the mountain it seemed proper to take a step back from the modern world into a simpler and less complicated one.

It occurred to her that Sam Stone had carefully chosen this life. Everything at his home was designed to keep his contact with the outside world to a minimum. The electricity, water, and much of his food came from his own land by his own labor. There were no television, radios, or other modern-day distractions that would let the outside world in. It seemed that Sam made his 'shine to not only provide his liquor but also to raise cash for the things he could not produce from his land himself.

Veronica wondered if she could be happy in his world or would her desire for a life of wealth and privilege beckon to her again? She had hated being poor but Sam Stone thrived in a world without so many material things. Then it hit her that her perception of wealth was only a means to take control her life and it was that control that she had always truly wanted. Her life with Roger had given her access to wealth but she had no more control over her life than when she had been poor, struggling along with her mother. Perhaps she could learn from Sam Stone just as her son was doing.

Sam took Teddy out to the chicken coop where he instructed Teddy on how much feed to take into the enclosure with him.

"We need to feed them and get the eggs," Sam explained to the boy. "Now I will warn you that the hens can be a little protective of their eggs, so the best way to get them is to throw some food on the ground to draw their attention away from their nests and then scoop up the eggs." Teddy nodded that he understood.

They stepped through the door and the chickens all began to cluck with excitement. Teddy grabbed a handful of the food, scattered it on the ground as he had been told, and watched as the chickens swarmed out of their nests. He watched Sam begin to collect the eggs and put them in a basket he had carried into the pen. Teddy started to collect eggs himself.

Teddy was just reaching into another nest when Sam said, "Not that one. Those eggs are the next batch of chicks. I have to have new laying hens every now and then. Go ahead and put the rest of the feed into the dry trough over there. See the faucet next to the water trough? Go ahead and let it run long enough to flush it out and then fill it to the top."

A few minutes later the chores inside the coop were complete and each of them had a basket full of eggs. They closed the coop and walked a little further until they came to the pigsty. Teddy wrinkled his nose at the smell as they approached.

"Yeah, they kind of stink but they sure taste good," Sam said with a laugh.

They opened a storage locker and pulled out the right amount of feed for the two hogs in the pen. Sam let Teddy put the food in the troughs and they watched the as animals devoured it. Sam checked the flow of water into the drinking trough and the mud that the animals loved to wallow in.

"Now what do we need to do?" Teddy asked.

"I need to go down to the still and check my mash. Would you like to run me down there on the ATV?" he asked as he watched

Teddy sprint for the garage, laughing at the boy's enthusiasm.

Teddy had already pulled the ATV out of the garage by the time Sam joined him. Sam slid into the passenger seat and pointed to the trail that led to the still.

Today, Teddy was much more comfortable driving the vehicle down the narrow trail. It was only a few minutes before they arrived at the building. Sam walked over, opened the door, and went inside. Teddy joined him as quickly as he could. The boy watched as Sam opened one of the blue barrels they had walked by the day before.

Teddy looked at the whitish looking fluid on the inside. He could smell something but he had no idea what it was. Sam dipped his fingers into the liquid and took a closer smell before putting his fingers in his mouth to taste it.

"Almost done," he opined to himself and then added, "I'll have to make a run tomorrow."

"What do you mean?" Teddy asked as he had no idea what the older man meant by "make a run."

Sam looked at Teddy and smiled before he said, "This is how I make money to buy things I can't make for myself. This barrel is full of what is known as mash. Mash is water, sugar, and grains that are cooked together. After it cools down a bit I add yeast to it and then leave it sit for a while. The yeast turns all the sugars into alcohol. Tomorrow I'll put the mash into the still and heat it up to distill the alcohol from the mash, turning it into some of the finest 'shine in the mountains. That's what's called 'making a run.'"

"Can I help?" Teddy asked.

"I'll talk to your mom about that but it will be up to her," Sam replied, then decided that he needed to have a little man-to-man talk with Teddy. "Your Mom is facing something that is very difficult for her right now."

"I know," Teddy interrupted, "That's why I want to help defend her from the bad people that want to kill her."

Sam looked at him and shook his head. "That's not difficult for her. She's at peace with what she has decided to do and you should be proud of her for having courage to attempt to bring down Percy Brigston," he said, then paused to emphasize his next words. "What's difficult for her is your having to grow up so fast."

Teddy looked at Sam, trying to understand what the man was telling him.

"You are unfortunately living in a cursed time that is forcing you to become a man before your mother is ready for it to happen. When I told your mom that I was going to train you to defend yourself, her concern was not about you handling a gun but being put into the position that you may have to kill a man," Sam said with all seriousness.

"I will never let them hurt her," the boy said solemnly. "Especially that man that's my father!"

"I don't doubt that but she is worried about how this will change you. She doesn't want you to grow to love death and violence or to accept it in your life. Neither do I," Sam said and then added, "Just tell her you love her and let her see you enjoy simple things."

The boy looked up at Sam and nodded that he understood.

Teddy drove them back to the house grinning all the way. Sam allowed the boy to park the ATV in the garage all by himself as he watched from the door to the house. Teddy exited the garage and closed it up before he walked towards the house with the baskets of eggs they had collected earlier.

They entered the house and found Veronica coming out of the bedroom while drying her hair with a towel. "You need to take a shower, Teddy. I left a clean change of clothes on the bed for you," she said in her best mother-voice.

"Okay, Mom," the boy said.

"Before you do, I need to show you both something," Sam said as he opened a set of cabinet doors that revealed several television screens that he turned on with one switch.

"I thought you didn't have television!" Veronica exclaimed with some confusion in her voice.

"This is not that kind of television," Sam said seriously.

Soon they could see the gate at the road as well as several of the switchbacks on the road leading to the house and parking area. Sam then switched channels and more trails were being monitored by other cameras.

"This is my security system. If any humans move along any of the approaches to the house there will be an alarm that sounds like this," Sam said as he set the alarm off and it was like a door bell chime. "If you hear that, we have company. When we return from town we'll go over what our plans for any unwelcome company will be," he said.

Teddy and Veronica nodded that they understood.

After Teddy and Sam cleaned up from doing their chores, they all loaded into Sam's Bronco and headed off to the Wal-Mart in Spruce Pine. They again passed through the tiny community of Little Switzerland but instead of getting on the Blue Ridge Parkway Sam followed route 226A. Veronica could not help but to be stunned by the views looking down towards Marion and South Mountain. A few miles later they came to a stop-sign as 226A merged with 226. From there it was a short drive to the Wal-Mart.

After parking the car, Sam said, "Welcome to Spruce Pine. I will let the two of you go get the clothes you need as well as any other personal toiletries that you forgot to bring along. I'll be over in the grocery section to pick up some provisions."

Veronica and Teddy went to the boys' section first where they picked out several pairs of jeans, shirts, and other essentials. Then Teddy saw the overalls.

"Mom, can I have a pair of these?" he asked with that pleading look on his face that made her give in much too often. She found a pair that would fit him and added them to the cart before she headed off to the women's clothing. It did not take her long to pick out a few outfits that would be appropriate for the mountains. The final stop was in the shoe section where they selected some work boots for both of them.

They then found Sam who had a cart full of essentials for his pantry. Veronica noticed that he had added coffee creamer, two cases of sodas, and two gallons of milk. They walked to the checkout line. Veronica watched as the cashier rang up the items. Sam reached into his overalls for his money but she put her hand on his arm.

"I need to pay my fair share," she said softly as she brought out a roll of hundred-dollar bills to pay for the goods.

When they left the store, Sam did not head directly back to his house but instead took them to a place called the City Drive-In that turned out to have wonderful burgers, Sam's treat. While they ate Sam produced two new smart-phones.

"This one is for you," he said as he handed it to Veronica and then the other to Teddy, "Do not use these to call anyone other than me. I've set them up so they will monitor the security system at the house. There is internet access but don't use it without discussing it with me first. It's unfortunate but the internet is monitored by people that Brigston controls and they can identify people by their browsing habits. I have no doubt that you are being targeted by those resources."

Both mother and son nodded that they understood that they had to be careful.

They headed back to Sam's mountain house but before they arrived he made them both check the security system to see if there had been any unwanted company. There had been none and they could see Diesel lying on the porch in front of the door keeping vigil.

CHAPTER 20 • GUITARS & GUNS

Sam pulled the Bronco into his parking area after returning from Spruce Pine. They unloaded the supplies and everyone helped to put things into their proper places. Sam then took the two of them into the lower level of the house. At the bottom of the stairs they entered the game room with the walls decorated with motorcycle memorabilia and photos of Sam and various bikes. In one picture there was a much younger Sam and an attractive woman.

"Is this your wife?" Veronica asked hesitantly, looking at the photo.

"Yes," Sam said softly. "Her name was Rosemary."

"She was very pretty," Veronica replied.

On the other hand, Teddy was intrigued by the pool table and asked, "Can you teach me to play?"

"I think we can arrange that. Perhaps your mother would like to join us as well," Sam said as he looked at Veronica.

"That does sound like fun," she said as she hugged her son.

Then something else caught her attention. In one corner of the room she saw a guitar on a stand with a banjo beside it. She looked the guitar over with great interest. Her mother had picked up an old cheap guitar when she was just a little girl and had taught her to play it. Some of her happiest memories were of playing the guitar while her mom sang.

Sam noticed her looking at his guitar and asked, "Do you play?"

"I used to but it was a very long time ago. May I hold it?" she asked and Sam nodded his consent.

Veronica played a few cords from an old folk song that had been one of her mother's favorites. Sam's guitar was of a much higher quality than the one she had all those years ago and the sound was superb.

"I think we might have to do a little pickin' and grinnin' session later," Sam said with a smile.

Veronica put the guitar down but let her eyes linger on it until she noticed Sam walking through the door to his office and now bedroom. Like every part of his house, it was highly organized and clean. There was a desk with a laptop computer on it. There were bookshelves with a few books and some small mementoes from his past life, including a picture of a very young Sam Stone in a tuxedo standing next to a radiant Rosemary in her wedding dress. There were also pictures of two girls that were obviously sisters and younger versions of Rosemary at various times in their childhood that ended with what must have been college graduation photos with their mother.

She and Teddy watched as Sam moved a small statue from one end of the bookshelf to the other. There was a soft click and then Sam pulled the shelf towards him and the entire unit swung open to reveal a hidden room. A light flickered on and they could see guns of various types stored on the wall. Below the guns were drawers. Sam selected two shotguns from the rack and quickly checked to make sure they were not loaded before he handed one Veronica and the other to Teddy. He then studied the selection of handguns and picked two identical guns that he also checked to ensure they were not loaded before he handed one to each them. Next he opened a drawer and pulled out six ammo magazines, which he put into his pockets. Finally, he opened two of the larger drawers and pulled out cans of ammunition. He opened one of the cans and put one more set of devices into the can.

"Let's go do some shooting," he said with a grin. Instead of leaving the way they had come in he opened another concealed door at the back of the hidden room, revealing a tunnel.

"This is so cool!" Teddy said with awe as they entered the

tunnel.

Sam followed behind after closing the secret door to his office and then the second secret door they had just come through.

"I want you to be aware that I have this hidden exit from the house. I always thought it might come in handy if the law got wind of my moonshine business," he said with laugh.

Teddy led the way for some distance before they came to a T in the tunnel.

"Go to the right. If you go to the left, you'll come out behind the chicken coop," he explained.

Veronica noticed the floor of the tunnel seemed to slope down. They walked for some time until they came to another door. Sam showed them how to work the latch and then the door opened into another concealed room. This room held Sam's still and other equipment that he used in his business. He pushed by them and opened the door into the still house. Sam closed the doors as they left the secret spaces behind.

"Now you both know how you can disappear if you need to," he said. "I have a shooting range just a little further on down the path,"

He reached into a filing cabinet and pulled out some paper targets as they left the building. It took only a minute to walk to his shooting range. They came to a clearing that faced a bank against the side of the ridge. There was a stand near a rope that indicated where a shooter should fire from. Two cables ran from poles behind the shooter's position to poles at the other end of the range. Sam walked over to a large table behind the firing position.

"Put the shotguns in that stand over there," he instructed and watched as they did as they were told.

After they rejoined Sam he pulled the magazines out of his pocket and laid them on the table.

"Now I want you each to put your handgun on the table," he instructed and again they did as they were told.

"The first lesson that you must always follow is to assume any firearm is loaded until you personally check it. The one thing you must never do with a gun is point at something that you do not intend to kill. Further, never put your finger on the trigger of a weapon until you are ready to fire it," Sam said in his best drill instructor voice.

Sam reached into his overalls and pulled out a third weapon that matched the two on the table.

"The weapon in my hand and the weapons on the table are Beretta M9s. This weapon comes with a fifteen-round magazine that loads through the bottom of the grip," Sam said and pointed to the bottom of the handle of his hand gun.

"I will now demonstrate how to make sure this weapon is not loaded. Point the weapon away from you and anyone else. First press the magazine release and remove the magazine, like so," he said, then demonstrated the process for them and placed the ejected magazine on the table. "Pull back on the slide and lock it in place like so," he said as he pulled back the top of the gun, ejecting a brass cartridge, and flipped the slide lock back in place. "You can see that there is no cartridge in the chamber," he said, pointing to the empty hole. "This weapon is currently unloaded," he finished.

"Now that the weapon is unloaded is it okay for me point it at someone?" Sam asked.

"Never point a gun at anyone you do not want to kill," Teddy said solemnly.

"That is correct!" Sam said and was pleased that the boy was listening to directions so closely.

"Veronica, I want you to demonstrate the process to unload your weapon," Sam instructed.

Veronica felt intimidated as she stepped around the table and picked up the handgun she had set down a few minutes before. She carefully pointed the weapon down and away from them all. She was a little clumsy trying catch the magazine as it dropped from the grip but she did and placed it on the table. She pulled back on the slide, which was a little harder than she thought it would be, but with a little effort the slide locked in place and she could see that the chamber was empty. She set the gun back on table, and stepped back to the other side.

"Very good! Now Teddy it's your turn," Sam said.

Veronica watched as her son ran through the process as if he had already done it a dozen times. He quickly finished and placed the gun on the table before he smiled at Sam.

"You are both doing fine. The next thing to learn is how to load your weapon," Sam said as he opened the ammunition box and pulled out a small device. "This is a speed loader. It will make loading each of the magazines easier but later I would like you to do a magazine just by hand. You need to be able to reload under different circumstances. The quickest way to lose a gun fight is to run out of rounds before your opponent does!"

Sam then demonstrated how to load a magazine as they both watched. He then had them each take half the magazines and load them. Then he had them unload one magazine each and load it by hand. It was much more difficult but they both managed to get the job done.

"The next thing we will do is learn how to release the slide and then pull the trigger. Please remember that even though we have just unloaded these guns we will treat them as if they were ready to fire," he emphasized before he picked up his weapon. "You will remember that we locked the slide in place by pushing this lever up," he said point to the slide lock. "After we place a magazine into the grip, we need to release the lock. To do so pull back slightly on the slide and move the lock down. Let go of the slide and the weapon is now ready to fire," he said as he again demonstrated the process.

He then turned and faced down the range while lifting the gun into a firing position with his right hand on the gun with his three lower fingers on the grip while his trigger finger rested outside of the trigger guard and his thumb wrapped around to the left side of the handle. He then placed his left hand over the front of the grip so that his left thumb was just above his right thumb.

"This is the correct way to hold this handgun. Take a good look so that you can do the same grip," Sam said and again mother and son watched closely.

"Take time to sight your weapon on the target by placing the front sight into the notch of the rear sight. When you have the target sighted, put your finger on the trigger and gently squeeze," he said and they all heard the click of the striker being released.

They then spent the next twenty minutes as Veronica and Teddy practiced releasing the slide and gripping the gun correctly, then dry-firing their weapons. Sam watched and occasionally stepped forward to make a slight adjustment. When he was satisfied that they had the basics down he proceeded to the next step.

"Ok, I will now demonstrate how to load your weapon. One thing I want to emphasis is that your finger never goes inside of the trigger guard until you are ready to fire. Is that clear?" Sam asked and they nodded that they understood.

Sam picked up a magazine and slid it into the handgun's grip with a click. He removed the magazine and made a point of showing himself checking the chamber before returning the weapon to the table.

"Teddy, it's your turn," he said calmly.

The boy then precisely reenacted the process of inserting and removing the magazine. He also made a point of checking the chamber of the gun before returning it to the table.

Somehow, watching her son helped Veronica feel more confident as she also completed the drill.

Sam selected a paper target and put it on the line, manually wheeling it out about ten feet from the firing position. He pulled three sets of earplugs from his pocket, put his own in first, and watched as his students followed his example. He then produced safety glasses and handed them around.

"I am now going to load my weapon like we did before. When the magazine is in place, I will release the slide lock like we did before only this time when we do so the gun will be ready to fire. I want each of you to tell me that you have completed this by saying 'hot' in a loud, clear voice. You will then take aim on the target, place your finger in the guard, and fire your weapon. You will continue to fire your weapon until the slide locks back. If you pull the trigger and the gun does not fire and the lock is still closed, you will continue to point the gun at the target and slowly count to ten. If the gun does not fire after your count, point the weapon down, pull back on the slide, and try to clear the round. Once you have cleared the weapon continue to fire until empty. If you cannot clear the weapon raise your left hand and I will come and assist you," Sam said as he prepared to demonstrate his instructions.

Teddy watched as Sam inserted the magazine into his own gun and released the slide.

"Hot!" Sam said in a loud, clear voice.

Veronica jumped as she heard the first bang, quickly followed by fourteen more timed shots. On the last shot the slide locked back and Sam removed the now empty magazine and checked to make sure there was no cartridge in the chamber. He pointed the gun up at the sky as he walked back to the table and laid the gun down. He then returned to the firing line to retrieve his target and replace it with a fresh one.

He returned to the table and he could see Teddy counting his bullet holes. There were fifteen holes within a five-inch circle.

"Your turn, Veronica," he said.

She picked up her weapon and pointed it up as she walked to the firing line. She inserted the magazine, released the slide, and said as loudly as she could, "Hot!" She sighted the weapon at the center of the target and moved her finger onto the trigger. She squeezed and the gun recoiled in her hands, which startled her. She quickly recovered and started to fire more quickly.

"Take your time. Breathe and aim your shots," Sam said.

Veronica realized that she was actually holding her breath. She exhaled and began to aim and fire more methodically. When her gun locked back she removed the magazine, checked the empty chamber, pointed the weapon up, and returned to the table. Sam retrieved her target, which had seven widely spaced holes. She waited for Sam to chastise her for the poor shooting.

"That is actually not bad for the first time shooting a gun. Just remember to stay calm. Breathe, aim, and then fire. Okay?" he said, then looked at Teddy and said, "Now it's your turn."

Teddy picked up his gun and pointed it up. He picked up a magazine and walked to the firing line. Sam put his target up and then ran it out.

"Take your time, son. You've got this," Sam said.

Teddy prepped the gun as he had been instructed and said, "Hot!" as loudly as he could. He sighted the gun and squeezed the trigger. While recoil was a new experience for him it did not break his concentration. He aligned his sights again and squeezed. His confidence was growing as each squeeze of the trigger produced a satisfying bang. On the seventh round there was no bang. Teddy remembered Sam's instructions and slowly counted to ten. He pulled back on the slide and the brass cartridge ejected. He sighted the gun and resumed firing at his target until at last the slide locked back. Teddy removed the empty magazine, checked the chamber and then raised his weapon to the sky before he walked back to the table as calmly as he could. His mother could see the pride on his face, knowing that he had done everything just as instructed.

Sam followed the boy to the table a few seconds later holding his paper target. Thirteen hits widely spaced.

"That's pretty impressive shooting there. Thirteen out of fourteen on your first time. You also did a great job clearing that misfire," Sam said with admiration for the boy who was proving to be a fine student.

"I think it's time to move onto the other weapon," Sam said as he walked over to the shotguns and returned to the table with both of them. "These are Beretta model 1301 twelve-gauge semi-automatic shotguns. They hold six rounds plus one in the chamber. Not near as many rounds but they are easier to load."

Sam then pulled the second ammo box onto the table, filled with shotgun shells. He quickly instructed them on how to see if the weapon were loaded and then allowed each of them to dry-fire the gun. Next he demonstrated how to load the gun, including how to put a shell in the chamber and then add a round into the magazine.

"Teddy will go first this time," Sam said and walked with boy to the firing line.

Teddy pulled the shotgun to his shoulder and felt the punch as he squeezed the trigger. He did not let that recoil deter him, again sighting the paper target and firing six more times. When he had finished, the target was nearly turned to pulp.

Veronica loaded the shotgun and took her position on the firing line. She had watched and listened to the gun being fired by Teddy. Now she was prepared and calm as she, too, shredded the target.

"I think we've had enough gun practice for today. Teddy, why don't you go get the ATV and come back for your mom and me," Sam said and watched the boy tear his way up the trail to the garage.

CHAPTER 21 • MUSIC

"**Y**ou and Teddy are doing fine on learning to use the guns but tomorrow you both need to practice firing both of your weapons and reloading them," Sam said as he and Veronica waited for Teddy to return with the ATV.

"Did you learn how to teach about shooting when you were in the military?" she asked, remembering just how thorough and precise he had been during their training.

"I guess we old soldiers never forget our training, since it's what keeps you alive when people are trying to kill you," Sam said as his eyes seemed to look off into the distance.

"Well, thank you for everything you're doing for us. We would be lost without you," Veronica replied just before Teddy arrived on the ATV.

"Go ahead and get in the passenger's seat, Veronica," Sam said as he placed the ammo boxes in the cargo bed and then climbed up into it himself.

Teddy demonstrated his skill at driving the ATV on the short ride back, wanting to assure his mom that he knew what he was doing and would be careful when he drove. It tickled Veronica to see him so serious but also enjoying doing something so grown-up.

When they got to the house, Sam carried the ammo boxes back into the house as Teddy and Veronica carried the weapons they had practiced with.

"Do you want us to take these back downstairs?" Veronica asked, indicating the guns.

"No, I want you both to load those guns and keep the pistols on you all the time from now on. You should also load the shotguns and keep them nearby wherever you are. You both need to remember that we may be attacked at any time and with little warning," Sam said as he headed downstairs.

Veronica watched as Teddy loaded the handgun and put the safety on with confidence. She did the same as Teddy picked up the shotgun and loaded it as well, including one in the chamber. Sam returned from downstairs carrying the guitar and banjo. He sat them down gently and then pulled two holsters from the inside of his overalls.

"These will clip on the side of your belt or pants," Sam said as he handed them each one. "Now let's get dinner done so we can make some music!" he added with a twinkle in his eyes as he pointed to the instruments.

The three worked together to produce a quick dinner of stir-fried venison with peapods, peppers, carrots, and onions from the garden, served over rice. Again Veronica was amazed at Sam's cooking skills.

They sat down at the table as Diesel joined them. Sam started to bow his head when Veronica reached over and put his left hand in her own and Teddy did the same with his right.

"Thank you, Lord, for the mercies you have shown us this day. Please bless this food that by your hand we have been provided," and as Sam was prepared to say Amen, he was interrupted by Teddy.

"Lord, guide us in defeating the evil men that want to kill us!" Teddy inserted into the prayer.

Veronica was stunned at her son's insertion into the prayer but then squeezed both of their hands and said, "Amen!"

"Thank you, Teddy for asking God for his aid," Sam said as he picked up his fork to begin eating.

"Who is God?" Teddy asked as he also prepared to take a bite.

"God created all things and is there to guide us through our time on this world," Sam answered while he lifted his fork to his mouth.

"If God created all things, why did he make bad people like my father?" Teddy asked.

"God did not make evil but evil exists because people disobeyed the way they were told to live by Him. Every day we all have a choice to make, to do what is right or wrong. If we choose to do wrong then we must make amends for what we have done. The problem is that to do that on our own we would have to die. Thankfully, God has provided a way for another to pay that price for us and that was his son, Jesus. Jesus never did anything wrong but he died on the cross for our sins. Those sins include what has happened in past, present, and future when we place our faith in God. It is still our choice every day as to what we will do but when we look to God the choices get easier," Sam explained to the boy that was quickly becoming a man.

"I'm not sure I understand all of that but I do know that I don't want to be a bad person so I will let God guide me," Teddy said as he dug into his food.

Veronica had listened to the exchange between Sam and her son and she was both reassured but also confused about what kind of a man Sam Stone truly was. She knew he had been in the military and it was obvious that he had experienced extreme violence, knew how to kill, and was willing to do so. He was also a man that exhibited total self-reliance in his mountain sanctuary. On the other hand, he confessed that he was dependent on God at every meal and was willing to share his faith in God with them. It was hard for her to grasp after spending thirteen years with the narcissistic Roger that a man that should feel superior to others was so humble.

After dinner, they all helped to clean up the dirty dishes and the kitchen before going out to the deck to watch the late sunset of the mid-summer evening. Sam poured himself a generous helping of his 'shine and then looked to Veronica who nodded that she would join him.

"If you would like a Coke, you may get one out of the fridge," Veronica said and watched the boy hurry off to get it.

"Tomorrow is his birthday," Veronica whispered. "He'll be twelve."

"We'll need to celebrate!" Sam said with excitement.

"Do you have pancake mix? Teddy loves pancakes," she said.

"I can make them from scratch and believe it or not I have maple syrup in the pantry," Sam said with a grin that Veronica answered with her own as Teddy returned.

"How about playing something on this here guitar?" Sam said as he picked it up and handed it to her.

Veronica held the instrument in her hands and lovingly ran her fingers over it. She began to strum a tune that Sam recognized as an old folk song called "Hush Little Baby."

As she played Sam began to sing with a deep resonate voice:

Hush, little baby,
Don't say a word.
Mama's going to buy you
a mocking bird.

Veronica joined on the next verse as Teddy looked on in wonder. He had never heard his mother sing before,

And if that mocking bird won't sing,
Mama's going to buy you
a diamond ring.

If that diamond ring turns brass,
Mama's going to buy you
a looking glass.

If that looking glass gets broke,
Mama's going to buy you
a billy goat.

If that billy goat won't pull,
Mama's going to buy you
a cart and bull.

If that cart and bull turns over,

*Mama's going to buy you
a dog named Rover.*

*If that dog named Rover won't bark,
Mama's going to buy you
a horse and cart*

*If that horse and cart falls down,
You[1]ll still be the sweetest little baby in town.*

Veronica became self-conscious as the song ended. She had never shared her music with anyone other than her mother.

"You sing and play well, Veronica!" Sam said with admiration.

"Sing something else, Mom!" Teddy begged.

"Sam sings pretty good himself. Maybe he would play and sing something for us," Veronica asked as she handed the guitar back to him.

"Ok, feel free to join in anytime and that goes for you as well, Teddy," Sam said as he started to play.

The tune seemed to be familiar to her but at first Veronica could not place it until Sam began to sing in his rich voice:

*I am weak but Thou art strong
Jesus keep me from all wrong
I'll be satisfied as long
As I walk, let me walk close to Thee.*

*Just a closer walk with Thee
Grant it, Jesus, is my plea
Daily walking close to Thee
Let it be, dear Lord, let it be.*

*When my feeble life is o'er
Time for me will be no more
Guide me gently, safely o'er
To Thy kingdom's shore, to Thy shore.*

Just a closer walk with Thee
Grant it, Jesus, is my plea
Daily walking close to Thee
Let it be, dear Lord, let it be.

Veronica and Teddy sat transfixed by his voice and the words that washed over them and then Sam said to them, "Come on and sing along!"

Mother and son joined in as they repeated the song.

When they had finished singing, Sam handed the guitar back to Veronica and then turned and picked up the banjo. He began to pluck the banjo and soon Veronica recognized the tune he was playing as yet another that her mother had taught her that was called "I'll Fly Away!"

They spent the evening playing tunes and occasionally singing and laughing. Veronica even took time to teach Teddy how to play a couple of cords on the guitar. She had never had a better evening in her entire life. It was getting late and she sent Teddy off to bed before she rejoined Sam to enjoy the music of the waterfall.

They sat in silence for some time but then Sam began to speak. "I'm glad that you and Teddy have found your way into my life. I never thought I would enjoy having anyone around me, again."

"We're glad that we're here too. You know that you're Teddy's hero and he hangs the moon by everything that you do. You're my hero too," she said and then wanted to add that she was falling in love with him but she could not bring herself to confess what she felt, at least not just yet.

He grew quiet again and then said, "I'll try to live up to those expectations but you need to know that I have seen some terrible things and I was used to murder innocent people. I came here to live with those memories, alone."

Veronica was stunned at his confession and also confused. It was impossible to reconcile his admissions of murder to the man that she had come to know in the last two days.

"I need to tell you about how I know of Percy Brigston," Sam continued and Veronica tensed at the mention of that evil man's name. "I took a job working as a spook for the government. My job was what we called 'black ops,' which means that no one is to ever to know what we did. I will not tell you any specifics because that would be breaking my oath but what I can tell you is that we killed people who were identified as planning to make terrorist attacks on the United States or our allies." He paused before he continued. "My last mission was to kill a rogue foreign military officer that we were told was involved in human trafficking," he said and then had difficulty continuing.

Veronica sat there stunned as she heard the words "human trafficking," having already surmised this was why Sam was familiar with Percy Brigston.

"My team and I discovered that what we had been told about our target was not true. In fact, he was the opposite and was fighting the actual kidnappers. We tried to call off the mission but we were betrayed. A cruise missile was used to take out the entire area we were in and was intended to kill us as well as the officer. I was the only survivor." Sam finished but he continued to look off at some distant horizon.

"Oh my God!" Veronica moaned as she imagined the guilt that Sam must feel over his men.

"It got worse after that," Sam continued, "My commanding officer said that there was confusion and that the missile attack was a tragic error. I felt that was not the case and I started to snoop around. I looked back at some of my previous missions that I then suspected of being based on fraudulent intel. My commanding officer found out and I was told in no uncertain terms to stop immediately. I was stubborn and wouldn't give up. I threatened to disclose what had happened on that last mission. It was then that I was approached by a foreign agent that I had worked with before. He told me that Percy Brigston had ordered the assassination of the target of my last mission. I was told that if I did not step down and keep quiet that my wife and daughters were to be killed."

Sam had tears running down his face at the memory of his personal defeat.

"The next morning, I submitted my resignation. It was only a week later that Rosemary was diagnosed. About a year after she had passed I moved up here to try and make peace with all that had happened," Sam said as he drained the last of the moonshine from his glass.

She got up and hugged him. She wanted to take some of his pain away but she knew it was his to bear.

"So, now you know how I know of Percy Brigston and just what he is," he said before he stood and kissed her on her forehead. "Good night. I'll have pancakes going first thing tomorrow."

CHAPTER 22 • TEDDY'S BIRTHDAY

The next morning Sam was up bright and early. He went up to the kitchen, started the coffee, and reached into the refrigerator to pull out a slab of bacon that he had cured earlier in the year. He got his cutting board and his favorite knife and began to slice nice thick pieces for Teddy's birthday breakfast.

Teddy was a breath of fresh air in his life. Through his eyes he was once again aware of the wonders of the world being discovered by an adolescent boy. It was truly a pleasure to let the boy try things and encourage him to succeed on his own so that he would become a confident man.

"The world needs more good men," he thought to himself. "And maybe I can help with that."

After slicing the bacon, he arranged the slices on a baking pan covered with aluminum foil. He then put the bacon into a hot oven. Next he prepared the pancake batter from scratch by combining flour, baking powder, sugar, and salt. He added melted butter, warm milk, vanilla extract, and an egg before thoroughly mixing. He put the batter aside and set up the griddle before pouring a cup of coffee for himself.

As he sipped his coffee he began to think about his biggest problem. Preparing Veronica and Teddy to defend themselves was only a minor tactical accomplishment. Defense would not bring down Brigston. Brigston's Organization was like the Hydra of Greek mythology. There were many heads but only one that truly mattered and that was Percy Brigston's power to control others through blackmail.

"The obvious answer would be to kill the bastard but that would not free those under his control," he thought to himself.

The key to Percy Brigston's control of others was the material he had on them. If that was not taken out of play then one of his lieutenants would rise up to take his place and the pain and suffering would continue unabated.

"Now, where does he keep that material?" he asked himself but when he looked up he saw Veronica walking toward the kitchen.

"Good morning," she said cheerfully.

Sam was just getting ready to reply when he saw Teddy walk out of the bedroom wearing his new overalls.

"Happy Birthday, Teddy!" Sam said and quickly added, "How many pancakes would you like this fine morning?"

"How many can you make?" the boy said with a laugh.

Sam quickly went to work and soon had a platter stacked high with fluffy pancakes. He had Veronica get the bacon out of the oven. Teddy had poured himself a big glass of milk and had put Diesel's food in his bowl.

Sam reached out and took their hands as they joined theirs at the same time and said, "Let us pray. Dear Lord, we give you thanks for this special day, for this is the day that we celebrate the twelfth anniversary of the day that you blessed this world with Teddy. We ask that you would guide him as he grows into a man. Lord, I also want to thank you for bringing Veronica into my life and the blessing that she has already become. We also pray for your protection and guidance in this troubled time. Father, we thank you for the bounty that you have provided us. Amen!"

Sam and Veronica sat back and watched Teddy tear into a stack of pancakes that would have intimidated a lumberjack. They quickly joined him and soon they were all stuffed to the gills.

"What would you like to do for your birthday?" Veronica

asked her son.

"I want to help Sam make a run today," he said and Sam suddenly felt a little odd since he had no idea how the boy's mother would react to her son's helping to run a still.

"What's a run?" Veronica asked, having no idea what her son was talking about.

"That's where Sam puts the mash in the still and makes the moonshine," Teddy said with a grin.

Sam waited for the explosion to come and tried to head it off by saying, "Teddy, I said that I would speak to your mom about that and that it was totally up to her."

Veronica looked at Sam and then started to giggle and then she laughed even harder to the point she had tears in her eyes as her son and Sam looked on, mystified. Recovering slowly, she finally said, "I am living in truly strange times. Yesterday I watched as my twelve-year-old son being trained to shoot guns to fight off people trying to kill us. Then he drove us home in an ATV. Today he wants to learn to make liquor. Any other mother would be having a fit but my first reaction is to tell him to have fun!"

"So, is it okay?" Teddy asked hopefully.

"Yes!" Veronica said with a grin.

"Good, because I could use a new still hand around here!" Sam said with a chuckle before adding while looking at the boy, "Could you take care of the chickens and the pigs this morning?"

Teddy nodded vigorously and then cleared his dishes from the table and stacked them in the sink before heading out.

"Do you have a present for Teddy?" Sam asked, arching his eyebrows.

"No, everything went up in smoke and there has not been an opportunity since this all began to even think about it," she replied and wished she had something for Teddy.

"If it's all right with you I'll slip out of here and go to the pawn shop over in Grassy Creek and pick up a guitar for him," he said with a wink.

Veronica almost knocked him over as she hugged him tight

and the tears welled up in her eyes. "Thank you, Sam!"

"I'll be back in about an hour," he said as he walked out the door.

Sam climbed into his Bronco and started down the drive. His mind returned to the big problem of Brigston. He needed to figure out where Brigston kept his cache of blackmail evidence. In today's technological world, the records could be digitized and kept on a thumb drive which could then be kept anywhere. However, it had to be somewhere that Percy could get to quickly and it had to be organized in a way to find what he needed easily. Then it hit him that there was a man who took care of all of Brigston's other critical records.

Sam began to smile as a plan formed in his mind while he was approaching the Mountaineer Pawn Shop at Grassy Creek.

Later that morning Sam pulled into the parking area at his house and in a short time Teddy came running out of the door.

"You ready to get to work, son?" Sam asked and watched Teddy grin.

"Good, I'll meet you down at the still. You take the ATV and I'll come down through the tunnel," Sam said and watched the boy sprint to the garage.

A moment later Teddy was headed down the trail while Sam reached into the Bronco and retrieved the small guitar suitable for not-quite-full-grown fingers from the back seat. He walked in and laid it on the table as Veronica smiled.

"I think we should give it to him tonight," Sam said.

"You keep him busy for a while because I'm making him a cobbler," Veronica said in a conspiratorial voice and smiled as she hid the new guitar away.

Sam went down to the still by way of the secret tunnel. Emerging from the second secret room, he carried the large copper kettle of his twenty-five gallon still. He set the pot on blocks that kept it level and above the propane burners. Teddy was sitting in the ATV and Sam was pleased to see that boy had his shotgun in the rack behind the seats and that his pistol was in its holster and clipped to the bib of his overalls.

"Come on back in here to help carry the rest of the gear," Sam said as Teddy stepped into the still house.

Sam had him carry the condenser while he got the thumper on the first trip. On the next trip he handed the boy a box of connectors and pipes while he carried a propane tank. With all the parts out of the room he closed the secret door and began to show Teddy how to assemble the still. Sam was pleased to see how quickly Teddy learned the task and was always willing to ask questions as to why the pieces went together the way they did. To Sam that showed a maturity in the boy beyond his years in that he not only was learning how to do the task but, more importantly, why it was being done that way.

"I think we're ready to put the mash in the pot. The important thing is to keep any solids from getting into the still. If that happens, they will scorch in the bottom of the pot and that will ruin the flavor of the 'shine. I want you to hold this hose as the mash comes out of it over this funnel that has a filter in it. If that filter starts to clog up you give me a yell to stop until you have cleaned the filter out. You got that?" Sam asked. Teddy nodded that he understood.

Sam started the small pump that moved the mash out of the barrel and into the still. He was careful not to suck up too much of the grain that had settled to the bottom of the barrel. Teddy watched carefully as the mash went into the pot through the filter. Then he heard the pump turn off and Sam came back out of the building. The older man walked over, looked at the filter, and then lifted it and looked down into the pot.

"Looks really good! You did a fine job. I never realized just how much I needed another set of hands doing this," Sam said with a big smile. "I think I'll keep you around for a while!"

Teddy swelled with pride at his hero's praise and couldn't wait to see what needed to be done next.

Sam put the cap in place on the still and lit the fire. Next he taught the boy how to make up a paste that they would use to seal the cap and other connections as the fire slowly warmed the twenty-five gallons of mash.

"Now we just need to sit back and wait for the temperature on this gauge to rise to around one-hundred-and-twenty degrees. When it gets there, we need to turn the fire down. Between that temperature and one-seventy is where the bad stuff will come out. We'll throw that away. After that we'll collect the good stuff," Sam said. "I think I'll let you watch the temp while I take a rest in my rocking chair."

Teddy watched the gauge and heard Sam softly playing a harmonica as he rocked back and forth in his chair. The sound was gentle but soulful and caused the boy to think. The night they had left Atlanta, his mom had said that their trip was to be an adventure. So much had changed in the last few days. He had to admit that the only thing he had liked doing in that other life was playing video games. It was through those games that he had escaped from what he saw around him. He had known that Roger was more than his mother's boss. He had also suspected that the man was his father. Even he could see that they looked alike. Roger was not a nice man. Roger mostly yelled at him and told him what to do at least until Roger had him packed off to go spend the night with the nanny.

He saw the temperature moving to one-twenty and said, "It's time to turn the fire down."

"Just turn the valve on the propane tank down till the fire is on low," Sam said.

Teddy felt the pride of having the older man's confidence to do things on his own. Compared to Roger, Sam treated him like he was a real person. Sam trusted him to make decisions and do things on his own. The older man would let him make mistakes but did not yell at him for doing so. Instead, he took time to explain what had gone wrong and how to not let it go wrong again. Even then there was more to Sam Stone. Sam believed in God and Teddy could feel that was what truly made a difference in his hero.

"We got a nice drip there. What's your temperature?" Sam asked.

"It looks like one fifty but it is starting to rise pretty fast," The boy replied.

"Let me know when you get to one-seventy," Sam said before he resumed playing his harmonica.

Teddy thought more about the differences between his biological father and Sam. Sam was who he said he was. He was a mountain man, self-sufficient, unapologetically Christian, confident and most of all, real. Roger on the other hand was dependent on Percy Brigston, in love with himself, paranoid, and most of all arrogant. Teddy wanted more than anything to be like Sam and, in that moment, decided that he would make that his life goal.

"Time to grow up," he said to himself. "At least a little."

"Hey Sam, we are almost at one-seventy," Teddy reported.

Sam walked over and confirmed that they were where they needed to be. He then changed buckets under the end of the condenser, pitching the liquid in the bucket into the weeds.

"Now we get the good stuff," Sam said as he stuck his finger in the stream and then sucked that fluid from his fingers. "That's some fine liquor!" he announced with a smile.

"Okay, Teddy, now you need to watch that gauge and let me know when it gets to around two hundred. If the bucket gets more than half full, replace it with this empty one," Sam said as he pointed to a spare bucket before he moved back to the porch and resumed playing.

It was about this time that Veronica appeared, having used the tunnel system to come down from the house.

"How is it going?" she asked with a smile.

Sam stopped playing and answered, "We're doing just fine. Teddy is a natural moonshiner!" he said with a laugh.

"I'm going down to the range to get my practice in. I need to catch up to my son's abilities," Veronica said with her own laugh.

Teddy loved his mom and was so happy that she was letting him do things that even Teddy knew were beyond any normal bounds for a twelve-year-old boy. His mother had changed in the last few days as well. All his life he had sensed that his mother was sad and afraid. That struck him as odd because just now he saw her happy and not afraid. She, too, was being changed by Sam Stone and this magical place.

Teddy noticed that five-gallon bucket was nearly half full so he changed to the empty bucket. He watched the stream of clear liquid and noticed it was running more slowly than earlier.

"Hey, Sam, I think this is slowing down. Is that what's supposed to happen?" Teddy asked.

"Turn the fire up about a quarter turn." Sam said before he once again played music softly.

He did as he was told and watched the flow strengthen. Again he felt the joy of being treated as an adult.

Another thought occurred to him. "Sam, may I ask you a question?" the boy said.

"Any time you have one just ask away," Sam replied.

"Do you think that Teddy is a little kid's name?" the boy asked.

"Not really. There was a great man that became President that was called Teddy all his life." Sam answered.

Sam then told the boy the history of Teddy Roosevelt. The boy was captivated by the account of how the man had overcome being a sickly child to being a cattle rancher, soldier, and finally President. By the end of the account Teddy knew that he would never want to be called anything other than Teddy.

"We're coming up on two-hundred," Teddy reported.

Sam came over and tasted the outflow and then said, "I think we got it done. Now we have to start the cleanup," Sam said.

"Maybe I can help do that, as long as you two men don't mind a girl helping out," Veronica said as she returned from the range.

Sam then showed them how to empty the remaining contents from the still and break it down, making sure to thoroughly clean each part before returning it to the concealed storage room. The last job was to gather some more buckets and empty the remaining grain from the bottom of the mash barrel.

"That will be pig food for tomorrow," he laughed as they carried the buckets to the ATV along with the two buckets holding the 'shine.

Teddy drove them back to the house where Veronica informed

them that dinner would be ready soon and they should come in and wash up after unloading the ATV.

When Sam and Teddy entered the house, they felt their mouths water as they were greeted by the aroma of spaghetti sauce simmering on the stove while Veronica cooked the pasta.

"Wow that smells fantastic!" Sam exclaimed as Teddy nodded his head in agreement.

"Well thank you but the two of you need to take showers before we can eat," she replied.

Twenty minutes later they all sat down to a wonderful supper of fresh salad from the garden, spaghetti, and spaghetti sauce made from scratch.

Before they ate they bowed their heads and held each other's hands. Sam said, "Let us pray. Dear Heavenly Father. We thank you for this food and the hands that prepared it. We also thank you for the blessings that you have bestowed on us as we worked today. Continue to watch over us and guide us in what we do. We thank you for Teddy and the blessing that he is to is mother and myself. We ask that you make him into a good man, Amen!"

Sam and Teddy devoured their food as Veronica felt the joy of knowing she had prepared such a delightful meal for those she loved. As they finished she went to the kitchen and retrieved the blackberry cobbler that she had made earlier. She placed a small candle she had found in the middle, lit it, brought the pan to the table, and watched her son's eyes light up. She and Sam sang "Happy Birthday" to Teddy and watched him blow out the candle.

After cleaning up the kitchen they went to the deck. Sam had brought out the guitar and banjo they had enjoyed the night before.

"I thought we might have some more music this evening," he said as he handed Veronica the guitar.

"That sounds great!" Veronica said but then added as she stood up and walked over to get Teddy's present, "But I think Teddy should join in."

Teddy was overjoyed as he took the guitar into his hands. This was a birthday he would never forget!

They heard the sound of distant thunder and Sam looked at the sky and said, "Looks like a storm coming on."

CHAPTER 23 • ROGER
GETS A BREAK

Roger Culpepper was an extremely frustrated man. Today was the third day since he had failed in his effort to kill Veronica Tillman. Someone had intervened with the skill that only a trained Special Forces veteran would have exhibited. Roger was incapacitated and his intended victims whisked away smoothly and efficiently. The only oddity of the incident was the fact that he was not quickly dispatched.

"Why didn't they kill me?" Roger said quietly for at least the hundredth time and still no answer came to him. That puzzled him because a professional never leaves loose ends.

In the intervening time since the attack there was no conclusive evidence of any particular person or group that had gained control of Veronica and the information she had taken with her. Just as bad, Dewy Wilkins' effort to identify who had attacked him was not bearing any fruit. Every time he talked with the detective he was told that these things take time.

On top of that was the fact that he still felt as if he had been hit by a truck. Every time he moved he was in agony. His phone rang and he groaned as he saw the call was from Percy Brigston.

"Hello, Percy," Roger said in the calmest voice he could muster.

"Has that police officer come up with anything yet?" Brigston asked and Roger could feel the tension in the man's voice.

"Nothing yet. He says that he has a whole team reviewing the security camera footage that they've collected but that it takes time. He had hoped that he would have some good footage from that school parking lot. Unfortunately, the camera had malfunctioned just before the end of the school year and it's not to be replaced until the end of July," Roger said, hoping the explanation would soothe the irritated kingpin.

"This is unacceptable! Someone is plotting to take us out and all you have is a bunch of coppers looking at blurry videos? I don't care what it takes, you must get us a lead! Bring in additional resources!" Percy Brigston shouted into the phone.

Roger had known Brigston for thirty years and had never heard him this agitated before.

"Yes, sir! Have your sources come across anything?" Roger asked and waited for another explosion but only heard a sigh.

"That's the worst of it, old man. There isn't a word or even a murmur about what happened and in fact it is as if nothing *has* happened. Whoever has her is keeping this all very hush-hush. We must find a loose thread in their cloth of secrecy and it must be soon!" Percy said in a more even tone that frankly was much more terrifying than his anger.

"The only thing I can think of would be to put out a story to the media that Veronica and Teddy have been kidnapped. Plaster their pictures everywhere and hope that someone will spot them," Roger said but his suggestion was greeted by silence on the phone at first.

"No," said Percy. "Or at least not yet. I'm still hopeful that we can discover who our adversary is and what their game is so that we may deal with them quietly. If we blast this all over, Veronica may fall into some honest cop's hands. Put more people on this right away!" Percy said as he ended the call.

"If one of our rivals has Veronica and the records, why have they not made a call with demands?" Roger asked himself and then added, "Especially with that video of Percy!"

His thoughts were interrupted by a knock on the door. He walked over and looked out through the peephole to see Dewy Wilkins standing there. He quickly opened the door and motioned Wilkins into the room.

"Have you got something?" Roger asked hopefully as he closed the door.

The crooked cop smiled and put a folder on the table. He opened it to show a blurry photograph of a man in bib overalls and wearing a black cowboy hat and a long bushy beard.

"Who is he?" Roger asked.

"We still don't know but this what we have," Wilkins said as he pulled out a picture of an old Bronco with a shadowy figure behind the wheel. "This picture was taken in the shopping center parking lot near where you made your grab." The detective pulled out another blurry picture of the Bronco on the road and continued, "And this picture was taken at a business on the route down to Saferight Preserve where you were attacked.

"So, what makes you think that this is the guy?" Roger asked as he was having trouble understanding the significance of pictures of an old Bronco with an old hillbilly at the wheel.

"I started to think about where else we knew the suspect might have been before or after the attack," Wilkins explained. "Then I remembered about the tracking devices and how they were put on those trucks to confuse us. I looked at where the trucks were headed and then tried to calculate where they all would have been at a common point at the correct time. There is a truck-stop just east of Greensboro that fit. I went there and pulled their camera footage and we found this," Wilkins said as he showed another picture of the Bronco at the back of a truck-stop parking lot.

The detective pointed to the photo and Roger could see a man in a cowboy hat along with a petite woman and a small boy sitting in the Bronco. He then moved to another picture of the man in the cowboy hat reaching under a truck bumper. Then the detective pointed back to the first photo he had shown Roger, which was an enlargement of the one where the man had been reaching under the truck.

"I'm pretty sure that's your guy that gave you that beating. We're trying to get a list of Broncos registered in North Carolina but we're not even sure if it's a North Carolina plate. I also have a couple of men canvassing the businesses at the shopping center to see if anyone knows who the guy is," the cop said.

Roger thought about it and suggested, "Get ahold of the tracking devices and see if there are any fingerprints." Wilkins nodded that he understood and walked out the door.

Roger picked up his phone and placed a call to Art Stanton, an Organization asset with a highly secret security agency of the U.S. government.

"Art? This is Roger. I'm going to send you a photo. I need your technicians to clean it up and put it through your facial recognition program. I need to know who this man is and fast!" Roger said and had not even allowed the man to finish saying yes as he ended the call.

Roger knew that Art Stanton had no way to turn down his request, not with what they had on him. He smiled as he thought of the treasure trove of dirty secrets that he carried on his person twenty-four hours a day and three-hundred-and-sixty-five days per year. Percy Brigston was paranoid that he would be targeted and had always relied on Roger to hold the evidence of so many people's indiscretions. Percy had instructed Roger to create the database in a way that it could never be copied without Percy inputting his security code. That code was only known by Percy. Roger had found that arrangement quite useful as he could use the information to get things done. Like he had just now done with Stanton.

CHAPTER 24 • PERCY'S PARANOIA

Percy Brigston ended his call with Roger Culpepper and felt uneasy. Roger was not being honest with him. Of course, that had never really bothered Percy before.

"We all have our little secrets," he thought with a smile. "That's what gives life its spice and has always provided me with the tools to build my empire."

It was truly an immense empire that in his mind rivaled the empires of Julius Caesar and Alexander the Great. Today, Percy Brigston could pick up the phone and any wish that he had would be granted. His library of secrets could bring down the powerful and humble the proud. His vast wealth could buy the greedy and foolish. It was not just powerful politicians that he held control over but also world media moguls, captains of industry, and the great thinkers of academia that were in his pocket. Most of them were not willing servants but rather his slaves that had been purchased by the currency of their own indiscretions.

"Yes, slavery has always been a good thing," he thought to himself. "It's the natural order of the universe. The weak have always served the strong and that's a good thing. All this modern thinking that we are all equal is nothing but balderdash. If the great masses of this world were ever left to their own devices there would be riots and wars until a strong man was lifted up to restore order."

Today was different. When it came to Roger's duplicity there was much more at risk. Roger had tried to hide that Veronica had stolen vital records that contained financial and personnel data that would destroy one of Percy's most lucrative enterprises, the one that provided cash to fund much of his clandestine operations to maintain his influence.

"No doubt Roger believes that my empire relies on the sex trade," he said silently to himself. "Roger has always been obsessed with adolescent girls," the old man thought with a grin. "I have a sweet tooth for them as well but Roger does not understand that he has only been managing a cog in my machine."

Percy knew that if he had to, he could shut down the human trafficking business for several years before the loss of that source of funds would affect his empire. He was confident that he could outlast any setback.

"I would, however, miss sampling the product," he said aloud with an evil snicker.

He let his mind wander on why Roger had not come to him immediately and then he began to let his paranoia take control.

"Is Roger Culpepper trying to stage a coup d'état?" Percy whispered as a chill ran through him.

The evil and extremely paranoid man began to put the scenario together. Roger used his lover and sent her off as a courier to one of Percy's rivals with just enough data to provide her bona fides. Roger would hold back the blackmail library as his hole card while demanding that he would keep the sex trafficking ring and the hundreds of billions of dollars in assets that it controlled. He would then offer to sell back the blackmail evidence in exchange for the service of a team of assassins to kill one Percy Brigston.

"I shall have to keep a closer eye on the man who would be king!" Percy said with a frown as he picked up the phone.

"Art Stanton here," a man's voice said.

"Ah yes, Stanton. This is Percy Brigston," he began.

"Yes, Mr. Brigston. I have the photo that Culpepper sent over and it will take us a day or two before we know who it is," Art

Stanton said trying to appease him.

Percy was caught off guard for just a second but then quickly recovered and said, "That's good. I want you to make sure that when you find out who it is in the photograph that you report directly back to me and only to me. I also have another favor to ask."

"Certainly, Mr. Brigston," the man replied.

"I am concerned about Roger Culpepper's safety. He was viciously thrashed the other day. I would like you to arrange to have him discreetly monitored from a distance. Mind you, he is not to be interfered with in any way but I would like regular updates on his location and whom he is in contact with. Is that clear?" Percy asked in his most gentrified voice.

"Yes, sir. I will get a man on it right away. I'll be in touch with you as I have updates," Art Stanton replied before the call ended.

"So, Roger must have slipped up somewhere. That must be why we have not heard from the other side. I wonder who's in this photo," Percy said to himself.

CHAPTER 25 • A TRAP
FOR ROGER

The morning after Teddy's birthday Sam was up early and got his coffee ready. Veronica also awoke early and came into the kitchen to join him in what had become their morning coffee ritual.

"Do you think that you and Teddy will be all right being alone until this evening?" Sam asked as he pulled out eggs to make omelets for breakfast.

"We should be. Is there something you need to do today?" Veronica asked.

"Yes, I need to fix our problem with Brigston on a permanent basis," Sam said as he started to chop vegetables to go in the omelets.

"Can't we just stay here where it is safe?" Veronica asked as fear of losing the sanctuary she had found here surged through her like a jolt of electricity.

"I'm certain that it won't be long before they know who I am and where you are," Sam began as he could see the tears well in her eyes. "The only way to stop them is for the people they control through blackmail to be more afraid of someone else than they are of Brigston. To do that I need to find out where the blackmail evidence is being kept and get my hands on it. I'm going to offer a trade with Roger. I'll give him back the video but he has to give me the blackmail files."

"Why do you think Roger knows where they are?" Veronica asked with surprise.

"Frankly, I don't know for sure but Brigston has relied on Roger to keep records and organize data for him so I figure it's worth a shot," Sam said as he started cooking breakfast.

Teddy soon joined them and helped to prepare some toast to go with the omelets.

Soon they all gathered at the table with Diesel sitting on the floor as Sam took their hands in the now familiar practice of praying over their meal. "Let us pray," said an unexpected voice and both Veronica and Sam looked at Teddy as he continued. "Heavenly Father, thank you for this food. Thank you for my mom but I thank you the most for Sam. Amen."

Both Sam and Veronica chorused, "Amen."

"Thank you for leading the prayer, Teddy," Sam said as he began to eat but his eyes flashed from Veronica to the boy. "I need to go away for a while today. Teddy, I am hoping that you could take care of the chores for me today. The animals need tending and we could use some vegetables from the garden. I also need the buckets moved in and out of the fridge. Do you think you can handle that?"

"I'd be happy to," Teddy said in a grown-up, matter-of-fact way that made his mother smile.

"You both need more range time with your weapons, too," he directed at both of them. "But the first thing I need you to do, Teddy, is run me down to the bottom of the drive to my barn after breakfast," he said and watched the boy light up like a Christmas tree.

After breakfast, Sam changed out of his normal overalls and donned a pair of jeans and a short-sleeved motorcycle t-shirt. He carried a vest and Veronica noticed that he had his nine-millimeter pistol tucked into an inner pocket of the vest that was designed for just that purpose. Veronica and Teddy gasped at the horrible scar that marred his lower forearm.

"Ready to go?" Sam asked. Teddy nodded yes.

As Sam started for the door he found himself being hugged tightly by Veronica who said softly as she held back tears, "Please come back to us."

Sam stroked her back and then pulled away. "I'll be back just as soon as I can," he said.

Teddy drove in silence as he maneuvered the ATV down to the front gate. He stopped by the barn and got out with Sam. He was curious as to what wonders might be in this other building but he was also wondering why his mother had gotten so emotional.

Sam opened the large sliding doors and the first thing Teddy saw was a track hoe. Off in one corner of the building he saw something covered with a tarp. Sam walked over to it and pulled the cover off of it. Under the cover was a black and white Harley Davidson Road King.

"Now that is cool!" Teddy said with admiration.

Sam disconnected the battery-tender and checked the oil and the tire pressure before he started the bike and allowed it to warm up. He then retrieved a riding jacket, helmet, gloves, and sunglasses from a small closet.

"Teddy, I'm going to be gone for a good while. I need you to keep an eye on things here. Make sure you have your guns nearby and loaded. Check the security system frequently. I don't really expect trouble just yet but I want you and your mom prepared," Sam said as he put his riding gear on.

"Yes, sir." The boy said but then he, too, hugged Sam.

"I'll call you when I need a ride back up. Would you lock up for me after I ride out the gate?" Sam watched the boy nod that he would and said, "You're a good man, Teddy! Always remember that and make your mom proud!"

Teddy ran and opened the gate and watched as Sam maneuvered onto the pavement before cracking the throttle and the motorcycle thundered away.

Sam thrilled at the feel of the Harley between his legs. He had become a passionate rider after being on a mission many years ago that required the use of motorcycles to get out after the job was done. That was one of the missions early in his career as a spook when his life was so much simpler. After his last mission he had spent countless hours reviewing all of his earlier missions to see which ones might have been complete frauds where he and his teams were used to commit murder for Percy Brigston.

He had determined that he had been used to kill or cause to be killed over eighty innocent people in all and the visits of the ghosts confirmed his assessment. Now was the time to bring the guilty to account for their crimes. He had considered killing both Percy Brigston and Roger Culpepper but had realized that the job was bigger than those two. He needed help because the entire Organization needed to be brought to justice and that could only be done if those that were being blackmailed could be freed to help or at least not interfere.

"Does that include Art Stanton?" Sam asked himself.

Stanton had arranged for his team and an entire camp of innocent people to be executed because he had been caught up in a scam to divert funding for weapons programs into his bank account. Sam had no doubt that what had happened to Stanton had happened to others as well. They were not innocent by any means but they were being coerced and would not have done service for Brigston voluntarily.

Sam decided that he would gladly let that type of people escape but Brigston and his willing servants had to be brought to justice. People like Stanton would surely rebel once they knew that Brigston could no longer expose them. It was his only hope.

Sam headed north from Spruce Pine on US 19E until he reached the turn off to Banner Elk on 194 that would take him all the way to Valis. He then traveled up US 421 until he could link up with route 88 just over the Tennessee state line. His plan was to ride to Mount Airy where he would acquire a throwaway cell phone to call Roger with. He wanted to conceal his true location and where he had traveled from as best as he could.

The roads he chose to travel on were not a route that anyone would normally take but on the motorcycle it was a pleasurable excursion. Just after lunch he arrived in Mount Airy. He parked on Main Street and was walking to Snappy Lunch to get a pork chop sandwich when a classic 1962 Ford Galaxy police car drove by.

After his lunch at the famous dinner, he rode over to Wal-Mart and purchased a cheap phone to make the call. He paid with cash and then rode north and east of the town until he crossed the Virginia state line. Sam pulled into a church parking lot to make his call.

He put the number in the phone and hit call. On the third ring he heard a man say, "Who is this?"

"My organization has your information, Veronica, your son, and most important to you, Roger, a video." Sam said calmly.

Roger Culpepper froze when the voice on the other end said that he had that video.

"What do you want?" Roger finally asked.

"We want all the blackmail records from Brigston," Sam said.

"What makes you think I can get to those?" Roger replied.

"Listen up, Roger. We know that you are the chief boot-licker for old Percy. You keep all of his important shit. Get us the records or we will send a copy of that video to Percy and we are certain he will make sure that you have an interesting but agonizing death," Sam said in the most menacing way that he could.

Roger agonized on his side of the call. He knew he was caught and had little hope of living through this if he gave up Brigston's dirty laundry file.

"I'd be dead even if I get that video back," Roger said and knew that it was true.

"Not if we kill Brigston. You can keep your little trafficking operation and the money but our patrons want out from under Percy Brigston," Sam said and waited for Roger to think through the offer.

"OK, how do I get you the records," Roger asked.

"Are they digitized?" Sam asked.

"Of course," Roger replied.

"There is a bar in Pilot Mountain called the Do Drop Inn. Go there alone and leave the thumb drive in your car on the floor under the steering wheel. You will then go into the bar and have two drinks, taking your time before you leave again. We will have agents watching your every move. If you do anything other than what I have told you we will send the video to Brigston."

"How do I get the video back?" Roger asked.

"We will get it to you after we verify what you are giving us," Sam said before adding, "You have one hour to be there!"

Sam ended the call and turned off the phone.

CHAPTER 26 • PILOT MOUNTAIN

Roger sat stunned in the chair of his hotel room. He had not expected the call from the other side to go the way it had. He knew they would somehow use the video of Percy and the girl as a threat but not like this. He had envisioned that they would take the video to law enforcement unless Percy turned over the keys to his empire. He had hoped that he would be able to negotiate with them long enough to locate their base and then have a team go in and kill everyone.

Now he saw that this situation was a golden opportunity for himself! If they killed Percy Brigston and left the rest of The Organization alone, he would be very wealthy and in a position to indulge his addiction. The loss of some of the blackmail assets would hurt but he felt confident it would only be a minor setback. He checked the time and realized he had to get moving.

A few minutes later he was driving as fast as he could to get to that bar in Pilot Mountain. What he didn't know was that he was being watched.

John Walters was following Roger Culpepper at a distance of several miles by monitoring a tracking device he had attached to the man's car. John had no idea why he had been ordered to keep this man under observation but as a spook he had learned long ago to never ask unnecessary questions. He was mostly proud of the service he had performed for his country but he was also a pragmatist that knew powerful politicians used the Agency and his services to settle personal scores. He suspected that his current role was likely this type of matter.

John watched as the man he followed turned onto US 421, which would take him through Winston-Salem's downtown. John decided to close the distance with his target to less than mile just in case he was about to turn off the main road but the target merged onto US 52 heading north toward Virginia and was accelerating. He let the target widen the distance to make sure he wasn't spotted.

Sam Stone had a much shorter distance to travel to get to Pilot Mountain. He had been to the Do Drop Inn on other occasions to have a beer. It was a biker bar with the normal types hanging around. Many non-bikers thought that the place was too dangerous to enter but the only trouble Sam had ever seen in the bar was someone drinking more beers than the wheels on their motorcycle. Bikers were for most part a brotherhood and you could count on your fellow riders to help you out when you were in trouble. He was counting on that assistance to give him a big head start back to the mountains. He parked his bike and went in.

"I'll have a beer," he said to the man behind the bar as he claimed a stool.

Nearby were several other bikers talking about their morning ride. The bartender put the beer in front of Sam and walked back to the other end to check on the other customers.

Sam turned and looked at the riders sitting nearby and asked, "Where y'all from?"

"We're from down in Lexington," a biker with a ponytail and a goatee replied. "What about you?"

"I live up around Little Switzerland," Sam replied as he shook the other biker's hand.

"There's some awesome riding up there!" another of the biker's replied.

"Yes, there is! What the hell you doing all the way over here?" asked the first man.

"I'm here to get my granddaughter back," Sam lied.

"What do you mean, get her back?" asked several of the bikers at the same time.

"She met a guy online who talked her into running away with him. She's sixteen and he promised her just how wonderful things would be. I tried to take her back a few days ago. We got into a fight and when the cops showed up he convinced them that I was the bad guy so they put me in jail for a few days. Then the bastard called when I got out earlier today and said I could have her back for five grand or else he would put her out on the streets." Sam said as he looked at the bottles of liquor on the wall behind the bar.

The other bikers became agitated as Sam told his story that, while not true, did speak to the nature of who Roger Culpepper was.

"What are you going to do?" asked a particularly tough looking biker that had been listening from a nearby table.

"Not much choice. I got some money and I'll try to buy her back. He's supposed to meet me here at two-thirty and when he gets the money he's supposed to make a phone call to whoever is watching her at a motel down the road and we'll go get her," Sam said as he sipped his beer.

"I got a better idea," said the tough-looking biker. "You go to the motel and get her and we'll take care of that asshole."

"What's this guy look like?" asked another biker drawn into the conversation.

"You'll know him right away. He's about fifty and he has a broken nose and two black eyes," Sam said as he started to pay for the beer.

"On the house, brother!" the bartended said.

"Then let me buy a round for the house," Sam replied and laid a hundred on the bar before he left.

Sam walked a short distance from the bar, then entered a store where he would watch for Roger Culpepper's arrival.

John Walters noticed his target's car slow as it approached the exit for Pilot Mountain. Again he closed the distance until he had a visual on the grey SUV. He then followed it until it parked at the "Do Drop Inn." He drove by and found a spot where he could observe the target by using his own rearview mirror. He watched as Roger got out of his car and went into the bar.

John was making notes of the target's activity when he saw a biker with a bushy beard approach the grey SUV. The man looked around before he opened the door of the target's car. The biker bent over and searched under the driver's seat. In an instant the man stood back up and then closed the door.

It was then that John recognized the man as an old friend, mentor, and former coworker!

Roger entered the bar and as soon as he was in the room every person turned and looked at him. He knew he was being watched. He walked to the bar and ordered a vodka and tonic. He was waiting for the drink when he looked up into the mirror just in time to see a man swing a pool que at the back of his head. Then his world went black.

Sam retrieved the thumb drive from Roger's car and walked back to his bike. He started it up and got ready to ride away. His route home would take a little over three hours of hard riding, taking him first to Wilkesboro and then on the same route he had used to take Veronica and Teddy to his place. He was just getting ready to pull out of the parking lot when he saw a man sitting in an inconspicuous SUV. Sam knew immediately he was being watched.

He rode by the SUV without looking at the driver and once he was out of sight, he circled back to get a better look at the man. He doubted that the guy was working directly for Roger or else he would have been confronted when he had opened the door to Roger's car.

"If we have other players in the game, I'd better find out in a hurry," he thought to himself.

Sam parked the bike and then quickly moved to where he could get a good look at the man in the car. As he looked around the corner of a building about a block away, he could see the man again watching the bar that Culpepper had gone into. He instantly recognized John Walters and he had no doubt that John had recognized him as well.

"Better have a talk with my old friend," he said quietly as he stepped around the corner and walked quickly to John's car.

Sam opened the passenger door and slid into the SUV.

"How have you been, Sam?" John asked as he continued to look in the mirror.

"I'm doing fine. What are you up to these days?" Sam replied.

"You know I can't tell you anything," the spook replied.

Sam sat there and remained silent for a while as he determined whether he could trust his former coworker. Sam knew that John had always been a straight arrow. At least as much as anyone could be that worked in the world of covert operations. He then decided he needed to tell his friend the score.

"Maybe I can tell you something. I suspect that you are observing the guy that was driving that grey SUV. I'm not sure what name you might know him by but his real name is Roger Culpepper. You don't have to worry about his coming out of the bar any time soon. I arranged for a little party for him in there," Sam said with a chuckle before he resumed. "Culpepper works for Percy Brigston running a human trafficking enterprise. He is looking for a woman by the name of Veronica Tillman who had been his mistress but then she discovered what a lowlife he truly is. She stole a bunch of records and he is now hunting her down to get them back and kill her along with her twelve-year-old son," Sam said as he examined his former coworker with his peripheral vision.

"That's all interesting but not my concern," Walters replied.

"One last thing you should know. Art Stanton works for Culpepper and Brigston. Art authorized that missile strike on my team and that camp on Brigston's order," Sam said as he stepped out of SUV and walked back to his motorcycle.

He did a lot of thinking on the three-hour ride back to the mountains. He had taken a big gamble with Walters and now he would have to deal with the consequences.

CHAPTER 27 • A SPOOK'S DECISION

John Walters watched as Sam disappeared around the corner but then felt the anger build in him. In his career he had done many things that were on the edge but he had never knowingly crossed the line between serving his country and going rogue. He had suspected for some time that Art Stanton was involved with operations that were off the books.

The first time that he had become suspicious of his superior was on that final mission that had killed Sam Stone's team. He had been ordered by Stanton to insert a two-man team to target a military camp that was being used to support terrorists. The mission had gone well and the strike was on target. He was just extracting his team when they picked up an emergency medical evacuation beacon from another team that should not have been there.

Stanton had pleaded later that there were conflicting operations that caused the friendly fire incident but Sam had shared with John how his team discovered that there must have been bad intelligence on the target. Sam then told him about being ordered to get close to the camp just before the missile attack was authorized. John had always suspected Stanton had tried to kill Sam's team to cover something up.

Since that mission John had watched his superior with an apprehensive attitude. Sam Stone's sudden retirement only strengthened those reservations. Now John would have to make a decision. Should he stay on mission, which would require him to report Sam's presence, or go with his gut and keep that to himself?

John picked up his phone and made a call that was answered on the second ring, "This is Stanton."

"Checking in, Art. The target has traveled to Pilot Mountain and has entered a bar called the Do Drop Inn. He has been in there for about twenty minutes," he reported and then ended the call.

"I wonder what kind of a party Culpepper is having?" John said with his own chuckle as he knew just how creative Sam Stone could be.

Roger Culpepper came to in the alley behind the bar. His head was throbbing as he tried to move and found that he could not. It was then that he could feel the duct tape that painfully bound his arms behind his back and was wrapped around his legs at the ankles and again at his knees. There was another strip of the silver tape over his mouth that wrapped around the back of his head. He was lying face down behind a dumpster. Then he felt other parts of his body ache from the beating he had taken while he had been knocked out. He also felt like he had been drenched with water but his sense of smell said that what had soaked him was urine. He was totally incapacitated but what he did not know was that his pants had been pulled down and a sign was taped to his back that said "Pedophile".

John Walters had waited for over an hour after Sam Stone had left before he decided to see if Roger Culpepper had somehow given him the slip. He entered the bar and found himself in a nearly empty establishment. There were only the bartender and one waitress who was obviously past her prime.

He sat down at the bar and said, "I'll have a beer."

The bartender set the beer in front of him and then started to wipe down the bar while looking him over. "Never seen you around here before."

"Never been here before," John replied as he sipped the beer.

"So, why are you here?" the man behind the bar asked with a raised eyebrow.

John wondered what happened to Roger Culpepper after he entered here almost two hours before. He was certain that no one in this biker bar would have been his friend. He was also aware that Sam Stone had retrieved something from Culpepper's car. John was also certain that Sam would have made sure that Culpepper would not leave Pilot Mountain with any chance of catching him.

"I'm looking for a man. You might have seen him earlier. He had two black eyes and an attitude. I need to find him," John said and watched the waitress leave the area.

"Now why would you want to find such a man?" the bartender asked as he put his hands under the bar and John was certain that the man was reaching for a weapon.

"A friend of mine is looking for him. He is about my size and has a full beard. He also has a rather ugly scar on his left forearm. I was with him when he got that about ten years ago," John said and watched the look in the bartender's face soften.

"Why should I believe you?" the man asked John.

"Maybe you shouldn't but that bearded man and I are friends. He would have died in that hell hole if I hadn't pulled him out. He and I have saved each other's lives more times than either of us would care to remember and tomorrow we would do it again," John said as he took a large gulp of beer.

The bartender walked from behind the bar and then towards a hallway that had a sign that said the restrooms were that way. He motioned for John to follow him. They walked to the end of the hall and through a door that took them into the alley. The man then pointed behind the dumpster. John could not help but laugh as he saw the humiliated man moaning face down behind the dumpster.

They then walked back into the bar where John sat back down and finished his beer and said, "You know that piece of trash can't just stay in that alley forever."

"I suppose not. Your friend told us what that asshole did with his granddaughter," The bartender said with a look of satisfaction.

"Perhaps I should place an anonymous call to the local cops and let them know that the man who assaulted my kid can be found behind your bar," John said with a smile.

"That should be quite humorous," the bartender said with a grin.

"I think I'll have another beer first," John replied and the other man howled with laughter.

About an hour later, John returned to his car, picked up his clean phone, and dialed the local police.

"Pilot Mountain Police Department. How may we assist you?" a woman's voice said.

"There is a piece of trash in the alley behind the Do Drop Inn. He likes to rape young girls." John said and hung up and then turned off the phone as he started the car and drove away.

After he had gone a couple of miles he called Art Stanton, "I lost sight of my target when he went into that bar. I did an investigation and found him behind the dumpster in the alley."

"Is he dead?" Stanton asked.

"No, but he did something that pissed a bunch of bikers off and the police have been called," John replied.

"Continue to monitor but keep your distance," Stanton replied.

CHAPTER 28 • THE RAZOR'S EDGE

R oger Culpepper was picked up by the police and then transported to the local hospital where he was treated for the beating he had taken. Everything was still a fog and all he could remember were pain and howls of laughter until the cops found him. He was now at the local jail in an interrogation room wearing an orange jumpsuit.

He heard the door open and looked up to see Dewy Wilkins enter the room with a uniformed police officer.

"Is he the one?" the man in the uniform asked with disgust.

"That's our man. He has a number of charges pending against him down in Greensboro," Wilkins replied as he looked the freshly pummeled man over.

"We'll give him to you for now but if I find out who this slime ball raped in my jurisdiction, I will want him back. We don't cotton to child molesters up here in Pilot Mountain," the uniformed cop said.

"You give me a call if you get anything else on him, Chief," Wilkins said as the chief unlocked Roger's hands from the metal table that was bolted to the floor.

Wilkins spun Roger around and none too gently cuffed his hands behind his back, which made Roger grimace with pain. He was then frog-marched out of the jail and into a secured parking lot. Wilkins then shoved Roger into the backseat of an unmarked police cruiser before getting behind the wheel.

"Keep your mouth shut while I get you out of here," Wilkins

said quietly from the front seat.

Roger watched as the car pulled up to a gate that opened electronically. Wilkins pulled the car forward to a check point with a second gate that remained closed. The gate they had just passed through closed behind them. A guard came over to the car and Dewy handed the man a folder that contained the prisoner transfer order. He also displayed to the guard his badge and identification. The guard went into his post and returned a minute later.

"Have a nice evening," was the only thing the guard said before he opened the outer gate.

They drove in silence for some time before Wilkins found an empty parking lot where he pulled Roger out of the backseat and removed the handcuffs. He then opened the trunk and handed Roger some clean clothes. Roger ducked back into the car and started to change out of the prisoner clothes.

"What the hell happened to you?" Wilkins asked. "I'm starting to think that you like getting beat up."

"I got set up," Roger said and felt his anger growing.

"From now on, let me know where you're going and I can have someone watch you. I don't think you're very good at this part of your job," the crooked cop said with a laugh.

"You need to remember your place or you will be *re*placed," Roger said as he almost had enough of the other man.

"If you do that, I might not tell you who that bearded man in the photograph is," Wilkins said.

Roger felt a rush of excitement surge through him. Besides the physical pain and humiliation of the last eight hours, he knew that he was going to die when Percy Brigston discovered that his blackmail evidence had been taken. Now he had a chance, a razor slim chance but still a chance.

"Who is he?" Roger demanded.

"We got some fingerprints off those tracking devices," Wilkins said with a grin. "His name is Sam Stone. He lives up in the mountains in North Carolina."

"I need my computer!" Roger said.

Wilkins returned to the trunk and brought Roger's gym bag and briefcase.

"I had to take thirty grand to dummy up your charges in Greensboro so I could get you released. I didn't think you would mind that," Wilkins said as he handed the bags to Roger. "I also went ahead and checked you out of your hotel. You need to get rid of the alias you have been using because that guy is about to escape and is wanted for sexual assault of a minor. You'd better stay out of sight, too, because your mugshot is going to be all over the place by tomorrow morning."

Roger heard what the dirty cop said but he was quickly trying to find out what he could about Sam Stone. He found that the man owned some property that was very remote but other than that he seemed to hardly exist at all. Roger then linked into a larger data base that contained people who had posed a problem for The Organization in the past.

He typed in Sam Stone's name and there was a full account of his background in both the military and as a covert agent and assassin. Roger noted that the man had reported to Art Stanton and had been involved in a mission that went bad for which he had been targeted for termination. That effort had failed but his entire team had been killed.

All of that was interesting but what drew Roger's attention was that Sam Stone had no known connection to any of Percy Brigston's enemies. Roger's mind reeled as he realized that he had been dealing with a lone wolf all this time. That was why there were no demands to Brigston. Then it occurred to Roger that he had been duped into giving up the blackmail evidence files but he now had a plan in mind. He needed some trusted men that could get to Stone's property, kill him, and retrieve all the things he had taken. He knew he needed to act and act fast before the pilfered information could be shared.

He looked at Wilkins and said, "I need a team to go after Sam Stone as soon as possible."

"Do you want him taken alive?" Wilkins asked.

"No, I want him and everyone else at the property dead,"

Roger replied.

"How many people do you expect to be killed?" the dirty cop asked.

"There should be three. Stone, a woman, and a boy," Roger answered.

"That's going to cost you big. I could get two others besides myself on short notice but I need a million dollars," Wilkins said.

"I'll have the money for you when they are all dead," Roger said as he closed his computer.

CHAPTER 29 • DUTY, HONOR & COUNTRY

Art Stanton sat at his desk after getting the most recent report from Walters. Roger Culpepper had been released into the custody of a cop from Greensboro by the name of Dewy Wilkins. Art already knew that Wilkins was an operative of The Organization and that as such reported directly to Culpepper just like himself.

Art had directed John Walters to resume his surveillance as he had been directed by Percy Brigston. That surveillance was now much more difficult than it had been when they had tracking devices on Culpepper's vehicle, which was now sitting in an impound yard in Pilot Mountain. On the other hand, Walters was one of his best agents so he should be able to keep tabs on the target.

"Yes, Walters is good but he's not to be trusted with the truth of his mission," Stanton thought.

Stanton had been walking a tight rope for over a dozen years. He now regretted his decision to be drawn into a scheme to skim money from numerous weapons programs. It seemed like such a sure thing. After all, with the billions being spent, who would notice a few million missing? Then one day a package was delivered to his house and in it was enough evidence to put him in jail for a very long time. The next day Percy Brigston introduced himself and explained that he might need a favor from time to time.

From that day on he had used the resources of the Agency to

do whatever Brigston directed. Memories of those things ate at him but the worst was when he had one of his teams targeted by a missile. Those men died that day and Art Stanton's soul entered the lowest level of Hell.

Art jumped as his phone rang and his stomach wanted to empty as he knew that it was Brigston.

"Stanton here," he said.

"Where is Culpepper now?" Percy asked.

"He is stationary in a parking lot in Statesville, North Carolina. He is still with that cop from Greensboro and they appear to be waiting there for some reason," Stanton reported.

"I want to know when he moves again and where he is going," Percy said and paused before asking, "Any news on that person in the photograph?"

"Not yet but I do expect a report from my analysts shortly. I'll call you as soon as I know," Stanton said, hoping to quickly end the call with the man who had brought so much dishonor into his life.

"I'll look forward to your call," Brigston said before the phone went dead.

Art Stanton stood up and walked over to his memento wall. He looked at a picture of himself dressed as a cadet back at West Point. He wondered what had happened to that young man who felt the commitment of duty, honor, and country. A tear formed in his eye as he again realized that he had betrayed all three of those standards.

He heard a beep from his computer indicating that a new intelligence report had reached his inbox. He walked over, opened the file, and was greeted by a familiar service photograph of Sam Stone and an enhanced version of the one that had been submitted by Roger Culpepper.

Stanton felt ill as he looked at the rest of the report, which documented that his analyst was one hundred percent certain that the identification was accurate. There was nothing else to do and it should have been done a dozen years before. He quickly typed a response to the analyst team that said this was all a drill and that they should delete all evidence that the test had been conducted. He congratulated them on their skills. He then deleted his own file.

Next he sent a coded message to John Walters that his mission was over and he was to return home. A moment later Walters acknowledge the order. Art stared at the picture of the young and idealistic cadet he had been as he reached into the drawer of his desk for his personal service weapon.

Seconds later his aide heard the shot that ended Art Stanton's life.

In Statesville, North Carolina John Walters wondered about being called off his assignment to watch Roger Culpepper. He was suspicious once again of what his boss might be up to. He was just getting ready to leave when another car arrived and parked next to the police cruiser. Two tough looking men stepped out of the car and walked to stand by the driver's door. There was a brief conversation before the men returned to their car and then both vehicles left the parking lot.

John decided to follow them for a while. He was just getting onto I-40 west bound when his phone buzzed with another coded incoming message. He picked up the phone and glanced at the message that announced Art Stanton was dead of a self-inflicted gunshot wound.

John called Stanton's aide. "It's Walters. I got the message on Stanton. I think he had me working off the books. Could you check on what my status is supposed to be?"

"According to his file you are on a training mission in North Carolina," the aide replied.

"Thanks. I'll let you know when I have completed my training. I would also like whatever intel we have on Percy Brigston. In particular, I would like to know his location," John asked and then ended the call as the aide said he would keep him up to date with the Brigston's location.

CHAPTER 30 • SANCTUARY DEFENDED

Sam Stone had been up all night looking through the massive file of documents that connected many wealthy, powerful, and influential people to their darkest secrets, the ones that would destroy their lives if they were ever revealed. It was a truly terrifying thought as to how much of society Brigston controlled through his blackmail.

Now he was focused on which of the victims he would try to enlist to bring down Brigston's empire. Sam realized that Percy Brigston had relied on his victims to spy on each other and inform on any that were trying to get out from under his control. He used the same process to continuously find new victims. What Sam had to do was to find the key victims that he could contact and tell that he had their information and would destroy it if they helped to expose Brigston. Brigston's entire Organization should collapse like a house of cards when a few key cards at the foundation were removed. Right now he was working through the media victims. He needed enough of them to create a feeding frenzy as evidence was released to the public. One of his problems in doing this was the discovery of just how horrible some of original acts were that the people were being blackmailed for.

Sam had his laptop on the kitchen table and was sipping on his normal mug of coffee. He looked up to see Veronica come into the room from the bedroom. Both she and Teddy had been happy to see him after his long ride back from Pilot Mountain the day before and frankly he was glad to see them, too.

"So have you made it through all the material?" she asked him.

"Barely scratched the surface. I'm trying to start with people that we might need to bring down Brigston but I have to understand what each person was being blackmailed for. I don't want to enlist the help of people as evil as the one we are trying to take down," he said.

Veronica nodded vigorously and asked, "Did you really have Roger beaten up by a bunch of bikers?"

"I certainly did and it went better than I would have thought. Take a look at this article I pulled down this morning," Sam said with a laugh as he turned his computer so that she could see.

There was a headline above a mugshot of Roger Culpepper, who was clearly looking like he had gone twelve rounds with the heavyweight champion of the world, that read, "Man in Custody for Sexual Assault." Of course the name in the article was not Roger Culpepper but that of the alias that he was using.

"They won't hold him long, though. There was no victim and I'm certain that he has resources that will get him released," Sam said. He remembered his meeting with his old colleague who was clearly shadowing Roger. "One thing I didn't tell you is that I was recognized near the biker bar by a man that I used to work with. I shared with him who Roger was and whom he worked for. I don't think he would give me up but if he reports my presence there it won't be long before we have company. We may have to leave here soon," he said and watched the sadness spread across Veronica's face.

"I'll miss this place, Sam. You have no idea how much I love it," she said as she looked up to him and then she added silently to herself, "But I love you more."

Sam looked into her pretty young face and realized to his shock what he saw. This young woman had fallen in love with him. In his long life he had come face to face with many terrifying things but what he saw in her eyes froze him to the core of everything that he was.

It was then that they heard the chimes from the security system. Sam instantly began to assess where the threats were coming from. He could see three intruders moving up the main road. He looked at Veronica and saw her pull back the slide on her nine-millimeter. She quickly ejected the clip that was in the gun, replacing it with a fresh one and then she quickly added another round to the previous clip before placing it back in her pocket.

Teddy came out of the bedroom with the twelve-gauge shotgun in his hands and his own nine-millimeter pistol strapped to his bib-overalls. Teddy was instantly scanning the security system. The three intruders continued up the road toward the house.

"We need to get into the tunnels. I want you and Teddy to go down to the still house. I will get behind them at the chicken coop," Sam said as he pushed them towards the stairs.

John Walters had lost the two cars he was tailing. They had turned off of I-40 onto route 226 going north. They passed Marion and continued north by what seemed like countless rock-yards and a smattering of other small businesses. They came to a stoplight near a Dollar General store. The other two cars turned to the left but John could not make the light. After his light turned green, he drove as fast as he could to catch up but the other cars had too much of a head start on the winding mountain road. He had lost them!

He called back to Stanton's former aide and the call was answered on the second ring.

"I need to know the location of the property owned by Sam Stone ASAP!" he said calmer than he felt.

As soon as the aide on the phone started giving the location, Walters knew he had made the correct assumption of where the men were headed. The question was, could he catch them?

◆ ◆ ◆

Roger, Dewy Wilkins, and Wilkins' two goons had parked by the gate. Roger had watched as the three men opened the trunk and quickly put on black flack vests and Kevlar helmets. Then they each took an AR-15 from the trunk before they closed it. Roger suddenly felt somewhat inadequate as they handed him a nine-millimeter pistol.

"Kill everyone," Wilkins said to the other two men.

The three men vaulted over the gate and began to move up the drive. Roger stood there for a minute and felt his misgivings grow. The man they were up against was not some criminal thug. He was a trained professional with over thirty years of experience. To think that he would just leave the main road to his lair unguarded was a mistake that would likely be paid for with blood. He thought of warning them but decided that they would make a great distraction while he approached from a different direction. If Wilkins and his thugs did manage to succeed, then so much the better.

Roger studied the road carefully and noticed a smaller trail that turned off to the right. He eased over the gate and moved quickly onto the path. The path soon became narrow and hard to follow but he continued to make progress. He stopped to check his advance and noticed that the main drive was at a much higher elevation and moved further off to his left. He moved ahead cautiously until he came to a wide stream where the water ran rapidly over large rocks. Roger noticed that there seemed to be stones that provided a crossing. He dashed across them and then on up the hill.

Sam, Teddy, and Veronica sealed the secret room off of Sam's office where mother and son each took advantage of the ammo locker to add clips and shotgun shells to their pockets. Sam set his shotgun aside and grabbed an M4-A1 assault rifle and a belt that held ammunition. He also pulled down an MK-3 knife and put it on the back of his belt. They then headed down the tunnel. When they came to the T-intersection they went their separate ways.

Veronica and her son quickly moved toward the still house. The plan was for them to stay in the concealed room and get behind cover. The first line of defense was that they might be overlooked and the attackers would then move away. If discovered, they would fire until they could retreat into the tunnel and make their way either back to the house or to the chicken coop.

When they reached the still house they quickly closed the door behind them and moved behind a table and sandbags. They assumed their firing positions toward the door to the still house.

Sam had moved quickly to the area of the chicken coop as he continued to monitor the three intruders charging up the drive. He positioned himself on a bank that rose above the road, took cover behind a downed tree, and waited. It did not take long before the first of the men appeared. Sam noted that the man was wearing a ballistics vest and a Kevlar helmet. He was armed with an AR-15 and there was a nine-millimeter pistol on his belt.

Sam was considering taking a shot when the other two men came into his vision as they moved from one covered position to the next on opposite sides of the parking area. The first man quickly moved toward the door of the house and never even attempted to open it but instead kicked it in before rushing into the house. As quickly as the man went in, he came barreling back out as Sam could hear Diesel's deep bark. The man took an unaimed shot at the dog but had clearly missed as Sam could still hear the dog continuing to raise hell while protecting his home. He knew it would not be long before the three men again attempted to enter the house and Diesel would be killed.

Sam carefully sighted the man furthest from the door. He put the sight in the dead center of the back of the man's helmet. He slowly squeezed the trigger until the rifle recoiled into his shoulder. He saw a red mist from where the man's head had been.

Sam quickly crawled away from where he had fired that first shot and a couple of seconds later a fusillade peppered the log he had fired from. He looked for his opponents but they, too, were hunkered down as each side waited for the other to make a mistake.

Roger was making his way up the path that was becoming ever steeper. He stopped from time to time to listen and look at what was going on around him. One of the times he did this he could hear a waterfall not far away. He was just getting ready to move again when he heard a large dog barking and then the sound of a shot coming from his left and up the rise. He wondered what was happening.

Roger rose and began to move faster up the trail. He heard a single shot and after a brief delay the rattle of rapid fired rounds from multiple weapons. He continued to move quickly and noticed that the path was not as steep and was now angling back to the left. After a short time, he came to what was obviously a shooting range. He quickly moved past the open ground of the range to where there was cover. He went just a little further when he saw a small building with a porch and a rocking chair.

Veronica could hear the sound of firing and knew that Sam was under attack. Her first reaction was fear but her second surprised her and that was an urge to go to Sam's rescue. Teddy was monitoring the security cameras and Veronica cursed herself for not doing the same thing.

She opened the app and quickly found the coverage of the parking area. She could see a body lying face down on the ground with a pool of blood under the head. She could tell that it was one of the three intruders. Then she nearly screamed as she saw Sam was taking cover near the chicken coop while the two remaining intruders were maneuvering to get around him. They would then be able to approach Sam from two directions. If someone did not warn Sam, he was going to be killed.

Veronica reacted and opened the door into the still house and dashed out the door before Teddy could tell her not to. She never looked to her left as she started toward Sam's position.

◆ ◆ ◆

Roger could not believe his eyes when Veronica appeared out of what he had thought was an empty shed. He raised his pistol and was lining up his shot when Veronica heard something behind her. She turned to find the battered face of Roger Culpepper looking at her.

"Time to die!" Roger said as his finger tightened on the trigger.

Veronica felt fear as she realized just how foolish she had been. Then Roger's head disintegrated into a red mist of blood and fragments of bone- and brain-matter that splattered into the woods. His body fell to the ground like a sack of hammers.

She looked to the door of the still house to see Teddy step out and calmly slip a replacement round into the shotgun's magazine.

"Don't do that again, Mom. I could see him on the security camera. We can go help Sam now but we need to move from cover position to cover position. Like this," Teddy said as he moved a dozen paces up the trail before taking cover behind a substantial tree on the right side of the trail. He then signaled for her to move forward after he had checked for threats. All those combat games he had played on his tablet were really paying off!

Veronica moved up the left side of the path and took cover about a dozen paces past her son. They continued to leap-frog until they could see the parking area, the entrance to the house, and the closed garage. Teddy pointed to himself and then up the hill to tell her he was going to try to get above the closest intruder and that she should come from below.

"How has my son become such an expert at stalking people who are trying to kill us?" she wondered as she began to run for her next position.

Teddy tried not to let his mind turn back to what had happened at the still house but it was hard not to. His mother had suddenly rushed out of their covered position even as he could see that his father was coming up the path from the range. He waited as Roger had stepped past the door while following his mom. He moved to the doorway where he could still see Roger preparing to shoot his mother. He had sighted down the barrel just like Sam had told him. His shot had been high since he had been aiming at the man's chest just below the arm that was holding the gun. Then the head of the man who fathered him exploded.

Several shots rang out much further away than the man Teddy was looking for. That had to be the other guy trying to distract Sam from the danger coming up behind him. Teddy pushed on but didn't rush his movements. He caught a glimpse of someone moving ahead. Then the man he was hunting stood up preparing to take a shot. Teddy carefully aimed his shotgun at the center of the man's back, squeezed the trigger and felt the weapon recoil into his shoulder.

Veronica also saw the man rise to fire on Sam and then watched in amazement as the man was pushed forward by the blast from her son's shotgun, but he remained standing. Now she could see Sam's back to the man that Teddy had just shot, who seemed undeterred as he took aim at Sam. She dropped her shotgun and pulled her pistol. She was aligning her sights on the back of the man when a string of automatic rifle fire erupted. She began to squeeze the trigger on her gun until sixteen rounds were expended and the man was lying crumpled on the ground.

Sam knew he was being stalked but he had no choice but to take them one at a time. He believed the man to his back was still not in position. He had the man to his front in a position to take a shot. He decided that a full auto would be best as the rifle would expend five rounds with one trigger pull. He took aim at the center mass of the man in front of him and pulled the trigger as he heard the sound of a shotgun and a grunt behind him. Just a fraction of a second later he heard the rapid but timed firing of a nine-millimeter pistol followed by something hitting the ground. The man in front of him was down. The whole incident was over in seconds but felt like an eternity to him.

Sam turned to see Veronica in a perfect stance holding her pistol while releasing an empty magazine, smoothly inserting another, and quickly releasing the slide lock.

CHAPTER 31 • AFTERMATH
OF BATTLE

John Walters was just getting out of his vehicle when he heard an explosion of gun fire up the hill from the parked cars. He quickly pulled his weapon and moved toward the sound of the guns. He knew he was in a difficult position as everyone would assume that he was on the other side. He found the same trail that Roger had gone up a short time before.

John moved like he had been trained to do and soon he was approaching the still house. He spotted a body lying on the ground and despite the damage to its head, he could easily tell that it was Roger Culpepper.

"Couldn't have happened to more deserving man," John muttered as he carefully scanned the path ahead.

He moved cautiously up the path when he heard more automatic weapons being fired and then a shotgun blast that was quickly followed by a combination of assault weapons and a nine-millimeter pistol being fired methodically. Then there was silence.

He moved with stealth up the path until it opened into a parking area. He spotted another body sprawled on the ground, which was wearing a ballistic vest and what was left of a Kevlar helmet. He then heard movement up the hill. He thought about staying concealed but he was going to have to announce his presence sooner or later. If the bad guys had prevailed, he could always withdraw the way he had come but he suspected that his old friend was very much alive and in control of the area.

"Sam Stone! It's John Walters! We need to talk!" John shouted into the air.

"Come out where we can see you! Keep your hands in the air!" Sam Stone's familiar voice replied.

John walked into the open parking area with hands raised as he had been told.

"Get down on your face and keep your hands stretched in front of you," Sam instructed him.

"Who is that?" Veronica whispered to Sam.

"His name is John Walters. He and I used to work together and he is the guy that spotted me yesterday," Sam replied in a hushed tone.

Teddy had moved to another position where he could keep the man in the parking area in a crossfire.

Sam hand-signaled the boy to stay put and keep Walters covered and then said to Veronica quietly, "Keep your weapon aimed on him. If he makes any movement, kill him!"

Sam kept his M4-A1 at the ready and pointed at the prostrate man on the ground as he approached. His eyes darted around to see if John had brought any company.

"I'm alone," John said as the weapon pressed to the back of his head as he felt his pistol being removed from his holster.

Sam quickly patted the man down and found no more weapons but did discover another two magazines for the gun he had taken. He then motioned for Veronica and Teddy to come closer.

"What are you doing here, John?" Sam asked as the others joined him.

"I was going to warn you about four guys that were about to jump you but I think you already know that. I also wanted to tell you that Art Stanton is dead," John said. "Committed suicide a couple of hours ago."

"Go ahead and stand up, John," Sam said as he absorbed the news about the man who killed his team.

"So, why are you not still shadowing Culpepper?" Sam asked after a minute.

"Because I killed him!" Teddy said which made both of the hardened men look with surprise at the boy casually holding the shotgun.

"Teddy saved my life," Veronica said as she looked at her son. "Teddy kept his cool when I panicked and tried to run off to help you, Sam. Roger somehow got behind me and was going to kill me when Teddy shot him."

"He did a nice job of it too. Most of Roger's head is splattered across the woods," John said as he looked first at the boy and then for the first time at the woman who despite being covered with dirt and sweat looked like an angel to him.

"You did what you had to do, Teddy. Always remember that," Sam said as he hugged the boy to him and then said to John, "I could use a drink, how about you?"

A few minutes later they were sitting on the upper deck and listening to the calming sound of the waterfall. Diesel had joined them and had at first looked at John with suspicion but soon accepted that his master's trust in the man was a reliable enough endorsement of his character.

Sam poured John and himself a generous drink of the 'shine that they were now sipping. Teddy sat close at hand practicing on his guitar. It was only then that Sam noticed that Veronica had disappeared.

Finally, John asked the question that was gnawing at him like an old hound on a piece of rawhide. "How are you going to take Percy Brigston down?"

"I have his blackmail evidence that he has been holding over everyone. I am thinking of how to use people he has been blackmailing to help destroy him. However, there will be a lot of work because I have found that some of his victims are just as evil as he is. Unfortunately, there is not much choice," Sam said as he stared off at the horizon.

"I might have another way," John said but then he heard someone come onto the deck so he turned to see who it was and he was stunned into silence.

"I have some lunch ready for us. It's just some sandwiches

so come on in and you can fix your own after we say grace," Veronica said as her eyes landed on John who was looking at her in a way that she found pleasing.

They all gathered in the kitchen where she had laid out various meats and cheese along with fresh sliced tomato, lettuce, and onions along with yeast rolls she had baked the day before. They all fixed their plates and then gathered together. John stood between Veronica and her son and across from Sam as they joined hands.

"Let us pray," Veronica said as she lowered her head, "Thank you, God, for bringing us through the trial of this day. Comfort us as we think of what we had to do and prepare us for what will come next. Bless this food to nourish our bodies in the same way that your word nourishes our souls. Amen!"

All of them joined her in saying, "Amen."

The next hour was spent enjoying their meal and getting to know John. John had been in the military when he was recruited into the "black ops" world. He shared very little about the specifics of what he did but in many ways he was a younger version of Sam Stone. Teddy and his mother could sense that the two had been in some tight places in their time serving together that had formed a deep bond.

John, on the other hand, was becoming ever more intrigued by Veronica. He found her extremely beautiful but even more, he found her intelligent and witty. He desperately wanted to get to know her better and had already pledged to himself to find a way to make that happen.

"This has all been quite pleasant but we need to do a little cleanup from the scuffle we had this morning," Sam said, rising from his seat.

"Let me give you a hand with that. You got a plan or do you want me to call in a team?" John asked as he also stood up.

"I would rather not have too many people involved just yet. I'm still not sure whom we can trust," Sam said.

"I'll help too," said Teddy.

"You don't have to," Sam said gently as he looked at the boy who had never seen the aftermath from a firefight.

"I need to do this. I want to remember all of this," the boy replied, knowing that this was a test of his becoming a man.

"If you don't mind, I think I'll take a pass. I'll get things tidied up in here," Veronica said as she began to gather their used dishes.

Soon the three men were out in the parking area thinking about what needed to be done. "I have a track hoe down in the building by the gate. Let's get the bodies into the ATV and I'll just dig a hole for them down there," Sam said without ceremony.

Teddy retrieved the ATV and they lifted the man's body out of the parking area into the back of the truck bed. Teddy noticed that man's face was nearly obliterated by the exit wound of the single round that had ended his life.

Then Sam and John took a rope up the hillside where they tied it around the man that Veronica had killed. They then pulled the body down to the ATV where the three of them lifted the man into the truck bed with the first body. This time Teddy could see where at least three rounds had struck the man in the back of the head and another that likely severed the man's spinal cord at the base of his neck. There were numerous impacts from bullets in his upper back on the vest as well as a larger shotgun blast in the man's lower back.

While he was observing the damage, the other two went to get the other body. This one was stitched with four rounds that passed through his vest and one in the center of his forehead. The man's eyes were frozen open and Teddy wondered if he saw his death coming.

"Okay, now let's go get old Roger," John said.

Teddy maneuvered the ATV down the trail until parking next to the body of the man who had fathered him but who had also terrorized his mother for the last thirteen years. He watched as the two older men dumped the body into the back of the ATV with the sound of dead meat.

They took the bodies down to the storage building under a tarp. Sam went in and quickly had the small excavator running and out the door. He moved the machine behind a pile of rocks and downed trees. He started to dig a hole but suddenly stopped and invited the boy over. He quickly showed him how to work the controls. It only took a short time before Teddy had a trench dug. Sam pulled the ATV alongside and he and John dumped the bodies into the hole without any respect for the dead thugs. Teddy then covered them with the dirt and rocks he had just dug out. Sam placed some of the trees and brush on top of the fresh grave.

"What do you want to do with the cars?" John asked.

"Let's take them to a couple of different spots and abandon them. We can leave the keys in them and if we are lucky thieves will steal them. Teddy, go ahead and take the ATV back to the garage. John and I will get rid of these cars," Sam said.

CHAPTER 32 • GOING TO HELL!

Sam had taken the unmarked police cruiser to the Blue Ridge Hospital parking lot. He left the keys in the ignition and the doors unlocked. He had previously abandoned the other car at a scenic overlook on the Blue Ridge Parkway. He had left the keys in it as well. For both tasks he wore latex gloves so as not to leave any fingerprints of his own either inside or outside the vehicles. He got into John's car and they began the return trip back to the house.

"Would you like to hear my thoughts on how to deal with Percy Brigston?" John asked the older man.

"Always willing to hear you out," Sam said.

"I think what you are trying to do is a waste of your time. I have a feeling that most of the people he was blackmailing are just as bad as him. However, one thing that they would never do is act on Brigston's behalf without direction from him. If he were to die and his sex trafficking were exposed, they would just keep low," John said.

"If old Percy were killed there would be some lieutenant of his that would pop up and make threats even if they did not have the goods on people. An investigation would be shut down and nothing would change," Sam replied.

"Not if Percy killed himself and at the same time there were an announcement that the U.S. government had discovered a world-wide human trafficking ring that was being run by the late Percy Brigston. His lieutenants would be too busy scurrying for their rat holes to make any threats," John said.

"And just how will the U.S. government make this discovery?"

Sam asked.

"I'll take the goods that Veronica took from Roger's office to the Agency as a national security threat. Those accounting and personnel files will be enough to bring him down as long as there are no cover-ups instigated before the public announcement and the outrage that is sure to follow. Art is no longer at the Agency to do that. I'm sure that you and I can check up through the chain of command to see if there is anyone else. If there is, we can do our own blackmail," Walters said with a mischievous grin.

Sam thought about John's plan and the more he did the more he liked it. "You and I will cover the chain of command when we get back home," he said.

"Great! Now tell me more about Veronica," John said with a wink.

When they returned to the house Sam and John huddled over the data base and searched for compromised individuals in the Agency. To their relief the only name that was associated with the blackmail file was Art Stanton. However, as they moved on from the employees they began to run into politicians who were in charge of oversight committees in both the Senate and the House of Representatives. There was also a troubling number of political appointees in various Cabinet departments that were under Brigston's control. Timing would be key to silencing any potential critics of the Agency.

"Time to start making some calls," John was saying as a knock on the door interrupted them.

They opened the door to find Veronica standing there. "Would you like me to bring you something to eat?" she asked.

Sam looked at the clock and realized just how late the day was getting and even more that Veronica and for that matter Teddy had not been part of any of the planning they had been doing. They were a big part of what had gotten them to this point and in fact both had taken a life. Sam knew from personal experience that killing a person, no matter how justified, was something that would stay with them for the rest of their days.

"Before we make those calls, we need to brief the rest of the team," Sam said and to his surprise he saw that John whole heartedly agreed with him.

Soon they gathered on the upper deck as the late summer sun was sinking behind the mountains to the west.

"John and I have a plan to end Brigston's empire. We've been clearing people we can talk with and tonight we'll arrange to have the records from Roger's office picked up. At the same time, there will be a team stationed here to watch over you both. John and I will be leaving with the records and be transported to a small island in the Caribbean. We will then take Percy Brigston prisoner for trial back in the United States." Sam said and cringed as he deliberately misled Veronica and Teddy on what was about to happen.

It was one thing to kill someone in a fight but to deliberately set out to execute a person was a different thing altogether, even if that man was one of the most malevolent beings in all human history. Neither Sam nor John wanted to put that burden on the young mother or her son.

Veronica listened to the basic plan and when they said that they planned on capturing Brigston she wanted to scream that it was too dangerous for them and that they should just send in a missile and kill him.

Teddy on the other hand just said, "Wouldn't it be easier just to kill him?"

Sam just ignored Teddy and said, "We have some arrangements to make so we're going back to the office. We'll tell you when there's more to know."

The first call was to the temporary commanding officer for the Agency.

Sam watched as Walters called and requested to speak with his new boss. It was a long conversation but to John's surprise the new commander had already found evidence that Art Stanton had been doing missions off the books. He had already concluded that some politicians had aided in covering up those activities. By the end of the conversation the new commander agreed to go along with their plan.

"The boss said he will have a team here in an hour and that the helicopter will take us to Fort Bragg." John reported. "We'll be debriefed on the material we're turning over. We'll have our kit awaiting us there as well as transport down to 'Devil's Island,' which will be the code name for Brigston's base. When we have made our insertion and confirmed that our target is present, we'll have two hours to finish the job," John said. "He has asked that you identify a dozen targets for raids to happen at the end of our two-hour window. He wants some perps to be paraded in front of the news cameras tomorrow. The boss is concerned that some of the politicians will start making noise if anything gets out while we're stalking Brigston."

Sam grabbed a notepad and quickly began to write down the names and locations of some of the worst offenders he had seen in the files. At the top of that list was Sidney Jenkins with the Charlotte Police Department with a note to check the files on all the local cops in Charlotte and Greensboro that were also owned by Brigston. He had also seen several places that served as holding facilities for the young victims awaiting to be sold and targeted those as well. For good measure, he added some of the holding facilities of sex slaves that were controlled by the rich, famous, and powerful elite.

They returned upstairs and found Veronica and Teddy on the deck where the mother was instructing the son on how to play his guitar. As with other new interests and tasks, Sam could tell that Teddy was demonstrating an ability to learn the new skill quickly and that he had the discipline to perfect that skill with practice.

Veronica and Teddy looked up at the two men as they stepped out on the deck. They knew it was time for them to leave.

"There will be a chopper coming in soon. On board will be a security team of six that will set up a perimeter until this is over," Sam said. "You two can go about your normal business. If everything goes as planned, we should be back in a day or so."

Veronica walked over to Sam, wrapped her arms around him

and said, "Please be careful! Teddy and I need you more than you will ever know!" She then kissed him on the cheek.

Sam then went over and gripped Teddy. "You watch over your mom," Sam said as Teddy hugged him tightly.

While Sam was speaking with Teddy, John walked up to Veronica and said, "When I come back, I would love to have the opportunity to take you out. You are the most intriguing woman I have ever met and I want to get to know you better."

Veronica was stunned but also flattered by the man's attention. She had been falling in love with Sam but so far he had never shown her any romantic interest. Suddenly her world was getting a lot more complicated. She then heard the military helicopter approaching.

They all walked to the porch and watched as the helicopter set down in the parking area with men in full combat gear stepping off the skids even before they had touched the ground and quickly dispersed. One man walked over to greet Sam and John.

"Hi there, Cap! It's good to see you again. Can you give me the lowdown on the situation?" the man asked.

"Good to see you too, Gunner. This is Veronica and she can give you the background and sit-rep. This young man here is my best scout and he can give you a detailed report on the ground and approaches," Sam said. The other man started to smile but then thought better of it as he saw the serious look on his former team leader's face.

"I'll make sure that I consult with them," Gunner said. Sam and John boarded the chopper and were whisked away.

The next several hours were a blur as they were moved to Fort Bragg where they received the gear they would need for the mission. They were then debriefed by an intelligence team on the basics of what had transpired and the material on the thumb drives that had been taken from Roger Culpepper's office. Sam knew that the intelligence team would spend months just beginning to understand the data. He then made the team watch the video of Brigston. Sam watched the blood drain from the team members' faces, despite having seen many horrible sights in the course of their military service. What they saw on that video would haunt them forever but would also motivate them to bring the monsters who willingly kidnapped, tortured, and sold children like cattle, to justice.

Next was the flight to Devil's Island where they did a high-altitude insertion. Sam was uneasy, being out of practice, but when he stepped out of the aircraft his training came back as second nature to him.

There was no intel on what they might face but what they found was a largely deserted island with a small village and a large main house. Sam quickly discerned that Percy Brigston had over-relied on his intelligence network for security without much consideration for even routine physical security on his island.

The two experienced black ops professionals had no trouble avoiding the few guards and servants on the property. They found an observation post and began to watch the routine. They quickly identified where Percy Brigston spent most of his time. Then Sam saw something that sent a chill down his back. Two guards appeared and were pushing a young teenage girl towards Brigston's apartment. The girl looked terrified.

Both of the black ops specialists began to move toward the apartment.

Percy Brigston was extremely angry. He had been trying to reach Art Stanton for hours and had not received an update on Roger Culpepper since the day before when he had learned that the traitor had been freed from incarceration at someplace called Pilot Mountain.

He was growing confident that Roger was on the verge of betraying him. Poor Roger had no idea of the extent to which Percy controlled the modern world. The modern world with its belief that all people had value. "What a stupid thought!" he growled.

People were no different than the beasts of the wild. All would submit to the real superior of any group. He had learned that lesson long ago when his parents always submitted to his demands as a child. When he was at university there was no doubt in his mind that those that came from the aristocracy would always be superior to the masses. As time progressed, he learned that most people were weaklings and would do whatever the strong wanted. Strength came from wealth and power. Wealth was easy and only required the accumulation of money. Power, on the other hand, came from controlling others.

This was where he had set his focus. He had learned that most people kept secrets that would destroy their power if those secrets were ever exposed. He developed ways to discover the secrets of powerful people and would then enslave them under threat of exposure. He then claimed their power for his own when it served his purpose. After that the world became his oyster.

"Someone is trying to take my power and it has to be Roger Culpepper!" he muttered to himself. He cursed his own weakness, as it was his trust in his record-keeper and problem-solver that had given Roger the means of betraying him.

There was a knock on the door and he grinned in anticipation of the personal pleasure he was about to enjoy. He needed a distraction from his problems.

"Come in!" he said and two of his thugs entered the room with a girl who was about twelve. She was clearly either northern European or perhaps North American. She was fair-skinned with light blue eyes and sandy-colored hair. The girl was trembling and terror filled her eyes. Her fear was what thrilled him as no aphrodisiac ever could.

"This is the ultimate expression of power!" he thought to himself as he motioned the guards to leave.

He walked over to the girl and lifted her face so that he could look at her better.

"Yes, she will do nicely. She might even please me enough to survive," he thought and then howled with laughter as the perverted anticipation built in him. "No, you will not see another sunrise," he silently pronounced.

He had just secured her bound wrists to a hook from the ceiling which left her trying to stand on her tiptoes. Then he sensed that someone had silently entered the room behind him.

He turned and saw a man in his thirties standing in the door and started to say, "What are you doing here, you fool, get..." but then could not finish. He felt something that was very much like the sting of a bee in his neck as a numbness began to spread rapidly through his body.

John walked past the crumbling body of Percy Brigston and pulled the girl's restraints off the hook. He then held the sobbing and extremely terrified girl as Sam removed the hypodermic from the neck of their target. It had been Sam's idea bring along the tranquilizer they had found in Roger's gym bag. Sam had explained the effect that the drug had on Teddy. He went on to explain that the victims were fully aware of what was happening around them but their ability to do anything other than breathe was completely suppressed.

Sam moved Percy into a straight-backed chair next to a small table, took a piece of rope from the coil hanging from a loop on his belt, and quickly fashioned a restraint that kept Brigston from falling off the chair but would have not kept him there without the effect of the tranquilizer. John moved to join him to lift the chair up onto the table. There was another hook on a beam over the table. Sam looped another length of rope through the hook and tied a noose on the end, which he placed over Percy Brigston's head and tightened around his neck.

Percy was aware of the noose being placed around his neck. His mind realized that the man who was stringing the rope was going to kill him and there was nothing that he could do stop it. He wanted to scream that he would give them wealth beyond their wildest dreams if they only freed him.

"What should I do with her?" John asked pointing to the terrified child.

"Go ahead and get her out of here," Sam said, checking his

watch. "Get her to our pick-up point. She's going with us!" Sam said as he secured the other end of the rope to the hook they had released the girl from.

Sam watched John and the girl leave and quickly exit the compound undetected. He looked at his watch, walked over to Percy Brigston, and softly patted his cheek. Sam could see the man's eyes had focused on him.

"Having fun, old man?" Sam said in a badly-executed imitation of Percy's British accent.

He then brought another chair to the table and sat down. Sam studied the man with the noose around his neck for a long-drawn-out period of time.

"We have a few minutes so we might as well get acquainted. My name is Sam Stone. A long time ago you killed my team and tried to kill me as well. That same day there was an entire camp of innocent people obliterated. There was one particular man in that camp that had been attempting to rescue children that your goons had been kidnapping. Among those children was his own daughter," Sam said as he again looked at his watch.

Percy vaguely recalled an incident that was somewhat like what the man described but he had ordered so many people who opposed his will to be killed that he was unsure. Maybe this man wanted something from him and was only threatening to kill him.

"You ordered that man killed for seeking his daughter," Sam said as he shook his head. "I did some more checking and found out that you had my team kill other innocents for your perverse purposes. Today you will be tried for your crimes." Sam shook his head then sat back and closed his eyes.

The ghosts came into his mind. He realized there were many more than normal.

As he studied the faces of the dead with his eyes closed, he asked a question, "How do you find the defendant?"

"Guilty!" was the chorus of ghosts but there was no joy or even vengeance in their verdict.

"What is the punishment for his guilt?" he asked.

Percy sat in the chair and watched the bizarre one-sided conversation and then he felt his finger move of its own accord. He then willed the finger to move again and it did. Perhaps the insane man who was watching him had used too little of the drug.

"If I can just get my muscles to work, I will be able to surprise him. Then I will kill him!" Percy thought as he continued to feel his body recover from the drug, "Just a little more time! Percy Brigston is not so easily killed!"

Sam opened his eyes and could see that Percy was beginning to come out from under the influence of the tranquilizer. He was fairly certain he had used only a minimal dose.

Sam stood up and walked over and released the rope around Percy that had held him in the chair.

"Even better you fool! In a moment I will turn the table on you!" Percy thought as he began to move his hands to remove the noose.

"Percy Brigston, you have been found guilty by your victims," Sam said as he paused and studied the man's face, "You have been sentenced to mortal death by hanging," he paused again and seemed to struggle. "If you confess Jesus as your Lord and Savior you will only suffer a mortal death but if you do not your death will be eternal. Will you accept God's grace?" Sam finished.

"Death is death," Percy moaned. He detested weak-minded Christians and his hope of escape rose as he realized that he could move his mouth and his hands were rising to remove the rope around his neck.

Sam kicked the table away and watched as the chair holding Percy Brigston dropped.

Brigston sensed his body falling even as his muscles continued to recover. He felt the rope quickly tightening around his neck. There was a jerk as the noose had stopped his fall but did not break his neck. The noose pulled tight and began to strangle him. His hands could not find a grip on the rope. He was being strangled by the weight of his own body. His fingers desperately attempted to pry open the noose but could not.

His lungs felt like they were on fire. He couldn't breathe. Blood thundered in his head as his heart attempted to pump harder to overcome the constriction around his neck. His eyes were bulging. Percy knew he was dying but then became aware that there were many people in the room who were watching him. He would give inconceivable wealth to any of them that would save him.

Then they all extended a hand and in unison said, "Guilty!"

Percy felt his bladder release as urine drenched his pants followed by only millisecond before his bowls released. Everything went black as the pain seemed to fade away.

Sam had watched the agonizing death. He checked Brigston for a pulse and found none. He then walked out the door and closed it behind him, then headed to the pick-up point.

Percy had no idea how long he had been unconscious but he became aware of a light. He wanted to go to the light but he could not move.

"Help me!" he cried out.

There was no response so he cried out over and over again.

Then he heard the word, "Condemned!"

The light went out and he heard the sound of people weeping and sobbing. Then he understood with perfect clarity that he was in Hell and would remain there forever.

CHAPTER 33 • VICTORY

Veronica had trouble focusing on anything since Sam and John had left on their mission. The security team that had been inserted around the house was nearly invisible but she knew that it was there. Teddy had met with the man that Sam had called "Gunner" and she had listened to him describe the property and pointed out on a sketch that he had made where the best locations would be to monitor the various trails and the road coming to the house. He then directed the team leader on the best ways for his team to redeploy under various attack scenarios. When he had finished, Teddy picked up his guitar and headed out to the deck to practice.

"Ma'am," the black ops team leader said, "Your son is an exceptional young man. He will be an exceptional leader in any field he puts his mind to." Gunner carefully folded the sketch that Teddy had provided and placed it into the pocket of his fatigue jacket, then left to rejoin his men.

It turned into a long night with little sleep for her as she found her mind wandering from one train of thought to another. She would think of Sam and how he had come into their lives, then pulled them into his. She had never been around a man like him. He was confident, humble, and approachable. He had taken her son under his wing and in just a few days transformed a shy introverted boy into a young man. She had been terrified at times watching the light-speed change in her son. She also knew that Teddy was now a better man than he would have ever been otherwise. Now she was worried about what would become of him if they needed to leave Sam's homestead.

Then there was John Walters. He had said that she was "the most intriguing woman" he had ever met. Veronica's heart beat faster as she remembered looking into his eyes and seeing the sincerity of that statement. Sam trusted John with his very life and that endorsement of his character meant more than anything to her.

"Men can be so confusing," she said to herself.

Her father had walked away from her mother and her before she had even been born. The boys she had gone to high school with were just that, boys. Then came Roger, who seduced her by offering her access to wealth and privilege. In the early days, she thought that they shared love but now she knew they both felt nothing other than the desire to use each other.

"Yes, I lusted for his wealth and power and wanted to make myself happy with it while he lusted for my body to fulfill his perverse fantasies," she said silently in her head. He had turned her into his personal whore. He kept her in her fancy cage but she was expected to perform for him on demand. She had been trapped for thirteen years. Fate had intervened when he left the door unlocked and she had flown away to find her voice. Yes, a voice that had ended his existence!

"But also, a voice that can sing again," she thought as she recalled the night of singing that they had shared and felt joy welling up in her.

Now she had met two men who did not fit the mold of any she had known before. Sam was like the father she never had. He loved her by seeing to her needs but he also encouraged her to grow and express herself. Most of all she knew that to Sam she was not an object but a person of immense value.

Now there was John. He shared so many traits with Sam but he had one thing that she knew Sam would never have; a romantic interest in her. Veronica wondered if their feelings for each other would grow into love.

"I want to find out!" she said out loud and felt a warmth in her soul.

That was how Veronica's night went as she struggled to find sleep until she finally nodded off sitting in a chair in the living room.

It was just after one in the afternoon when there was a knock on the door. Veronica watched as Teddy drew his pistol and walked to the door where he cautiously checked on who was knocking. She saw him relax as he opened the door for Gunner to come in.

"Ma'am, I have been instructed to have you join a secured briefing via a satellite link," he said as he pulled a tablet from his haversack. He set it up on the table and then typed on the keyboard until the screen display lit up. A man about Sam's age wearing an expensive suit came on.

"Ms. Tillman, my name is Howard Passage. I am John Walters' acting commander and an old acquaintance of Sam Stone," the man said and paused before continuing. "Thanks to the information you provided we have conducted numerous raids today," he paused again as the screen began to show news footage from many places around the country.

There was a scene in which thirty girls between the ages of ten and fourteen were being escorted by police officers away from a warehouse-type structure. That was followed by footage of three men and a woman being walked into a jail while wearing handcuffs and shackles. One of the men had an eye that was swollen closed. The coverage shifted and there was a scene of a man being walked in front of the press with a caption below that said "Long Time Charlotte Police Lieutenant Sidney Jenkins Charged." The news coverage continued with captions that referred to corruption, child prostitution, human trafficking, and even worse.

Then came the finale. The captions now said things like "Wealthy Social Trendsetter Implicated" or "Influential Billionaire Ringleader!" and finally "Percy Brigston, Pimp." There was widespread speculation as to who else was directly involved or had covered up the man's crimes. Then there was the final caption with a picture of Percy Brigston that said "Dead from Apparent Suicide."

The screen returned to Howard Passage looking grim but satisfied.

"I wanted to share with you that Sam and John are safe and on their way back to you. They have done a great service for their country," he said with a smile. "And you have done an even greater service to so many children that have been forced into unimaginable suffering." He paused again and Veronica could see tears glistening in the old warrior's eyes. "I have dedicated my life to fighting those that traffic in evil but you, my lady, have exceeded all of my efforts and I'll never be able to surpass your achievement. I salute you for what you have done and you will be my hero until my dying day." The image of the man faded as he snapped a salute to Veronica.

Gunner walked up to her and shook her hand. "My team will leave when Sam and John arrive. Not much need for us here with those two and young Teddy around!" he said with a smile, then stood at attention and added, "It has been a privilege and an honor to have served you!"

Veronica turned to see Teddy standing nearby bursting with pride in his mother and the risks she had taken to end the suffering of so many. A few minutes later they heard and felt the deep thumping of a helicopter's rotor blades getting louder and louder. They stepped out onto the porch and watched as the aircraft hovered and turned before landing. Sam and John stepped out of the aircraft but they were not alone. Between them there was a small girl with straight blonde hair and light blue eyes. She was desperately clinging to John's arm with both of her hands.

The security team quickly boarded the helicopter while Sam, John, and the girl joined Veronica and Teddy on the porch to watch and wave as the chopper lifted off and disappeared over the ridge.

"This is Nadia," John said as he looked at Veronica.

Veronica bent to look the girl in her eyes and said, "You're safe now!"

Nadia melted into Veronica's arms and softly began to cry. She could only understand a few words of English but she knew that she was now out of danger.

"I could use a drink about now. How about you, John?" Sam asked as the entered the house.

"Do you have any more of that 'shine?" John replied. Sam and Teddy looked at each other and burst out laughing.

A short time later the two of them were sitting on the deck sipping their drinks. Teddy sat nearby strumming his guitar and Sam could tell that the boy was learning fast. Veronica had taken Nadia inside to help her clean up and to find her some clean clothes.

"So, what are you going to do now?" Sam asked John.

"I think I'm going to quite the Agency," John replied.

"Then what?" Sam asked.

"If we can't find Nadia's parents, I'm going to adopt her. I guess I believe that old adage that if you save a person's life that they become your responsibility for all time," John replied again as he looked off to the far horizon.

"Might be kind of hard to get that adoption done as an unemployed single man," Sam commented before he took another sip of his homemade whisky.

"True enough," John replied and seemed to think about something for a protracted period of time before he said. "I am kind of thinking of courting Veronica. That is, as long as you and Teddy give your blessing for me to do so." Sam grinned as he nodded his approval. Teddy stopped picking the guitar and smiled his own consent.

"As for employment, I'm thinking about taking up moonshining if you would be willing to teach me and if not, I'm sure I will find something else to do," John said with a raised eyebrow.

"I think I might need a bigger still or maybe we should just go legal and start a distillery. How does Toe River Distillery sound?" Sam said with a big grin.

"Not bad at all. Here is to the new and totally unstoppable Toe River Distillery!" John said as he lifted his glass in a toast to which Sam responded in kind.

"You're also going to need a house of your own if you're going to have these children about. I happen to own some more acreage a few miles away. I'll bet the three of us could get something built in no time," Sam said as he picked up his own guitar and started to play in harmony with Teddy's tune.

Later that night everyone had settled in. Veronica and Nadia were in Sam's bed while John and Teddy had moved down to the still house with a couple of hammocks. Sam now sat on the deck with Diesel as his only companion, listening to the comforting sound of the waterfall.

It didn't surprise him when the ghost materialized in the chair beside him.

"Higgins, it's good to see you," he said softly as the fireflies strobed on and off in the cool night air.

"I came to say goodbye, Cap," the ghost said.

"I know and I want to thank you for helping me to forgive myself," Sam said as he felt the burden he had carried for so long lift from his shoulders.

"You're a good man and always have been!" the ghost said as it evaporated like a mist in the morning sun.

EPILOG

Veronica was having trouble breathing as her nerves stood on end. Sam stood nearby and gave her a reassuring smile as he extended his hand and pulled her right arm over his left.

"You look beautiful, sweetheart," he said quietly as he turned and gave her a fatherly kiss on her cheek.

"You look very dashing yourself, Dad," Veronica replied as they looked into a mirror at Geneva Hall to see the reflection of Veronica in her stunning wedding dress and Sam in his black tuxedo.

It had been over a year since they had met in that desperate time. She had fallen deeply in love with John Walters and today they would be joined as husband and wife. She tried not to think of her life before she had come to the Blue Ridge Mountains of southern Appalachia, but she had come to understand that while the Devil had intended those years to destroy her, God had turned them into preparation for the life that was to come.

So many good things had come out of those times. She had a father now in Sam. She had another man who truly loved her and they would spend the rest of their time in this temporal world together. She had her son who continued to grow into the most amazing young man and she now had a daughter in Nadia who had no family back where she had come from. They had found out that Nadia had been orphaned and a street urchin who had been scooped up and sold off to Percy Brigston's evil Organization. Veronica had also come into her own in the last year as she began to serve as a counselor for women trying to escape domestic violence.

All of those things were wonderful but the most amazing thing that had happened, as far as Veronica was concerned, was the personal relationship that she now had with God. She knew that God would always be with her and she could now face whatever tomorrow might bring.

"It's time," Sam said as he led her on the short walk to the Church of The Resurrection, the small chapel next door to Geneva Hall. They would return to Geneva Hall for the wedding reception after the ceremony.

Standing at the door of the chapel was Nadia, looking stunning in her light blue Maid of Honor dress. Her blonde locks were braided into a stylish hairdo that accented her beautiful face and her slender neck, which was adorned with a heart-shaped pendent with a single diamond set in it. Veronica smiled as she thought about the diamond and its origin.

"You look stunning Momma!" the girl said in her heavily accented English.

Sam then opened the door and allowed Nadia to precede them while holding her own small bouquet of flowers. When Veronica stepped over the threshold of the church and the pianist began to play "Love Devine, All Loves Excelling," the guests rose and turned to look at her. It was not a big wedding but there were guests on both sides of the aisle. On her side were two pews filled with men in full dress military uniform who had been on her security team as well as Gunner and Howard Passage. There were also people who worked with her at the shelter for abused women but the most special person was her mother, from whom she had been cut off years ago as part of Roger's effort to isolate and control her.

Veronica took in all of that in one quick look but where her eyes landed was on John, who wore a white tuxedo and was so handsome that it made her blush with desire. Standing next to her husband-to-be was Teddy in his black tuxedo, smiling broadly as she approached. Sam escorted her to the left side of the alter where they stopped just short of where Nadia took her position, as the processional music softened and faded out.

"Please be seated," the pastor said. "We are gathered here today to join in holy matrimony Veronica Tillman and John Walters. Who gives Veronica to be married?"

Veronica's mother stood and joined her on her left side as Sam remained on her right and they both said, "We do!" and each kissed her on the cheek before returning to the front pew.

Veronica felt as if she were in a dream as the pastor proceeded to instruct them on what God had decreed a marriage to be and he asked if they would pledge to keep their marriage in agreement with God's plan. When they exchanged vows she was terrified that she would make a mistake but as she began to pledge her vows to John the words came easily and without hesitation. Likewise, John looked her deeply in her eyes and pledged himself to her. They then placed the rings that Teddy handed them at the proper moment onto each other's fingers.

The pastor had them turn to face their guests and said, "Ladies and Gentlemen it is with great honor that I introduce to you Mr. and Mrs. John Walters! You may kiss the bride!"

As Veronica returned her husband's kiss she looked forward with excitement and anticipation to the journey they were only beginning.

The End

AFTERWORD

I would like to thank you for reading my first novel!

The task of writing was an exciting experience of taking a vague story idea and then breathing life into it. As an author I had the great joy of creating characters. Each one was formed with basic ideas that fit into the storyline but then they each transformed into relatable personalities such as woman trapped by a bad life decision or a man who is confronted by the fact that he had been used to commit evil.

The next challenge faced by a new author is the entire process of learning how to get the work published. This requires many hours of reading articles from other aspiring writers as well as some truly boring legal disclosures.

Then there are countless decisions that must be made as to where to spend one's limited budget. That is right! It cost money to publish a book. Cover design, editing services and promotional strategies can be very expensive but necessary to get a book into the hands of people like yourself. But in the end that is the objective.

I truly hope that you enjoyed my story and if you did, please leave a review where you purchased the book. I promise that I will read every one of them.

To stay informed on future books you may find me on Facebook or Goodreads.

ABOUT THE AUTHOR

Michael Rodney Moore

Mike and his wife Debbie live in the mountains of North Carolina. He started to write after retiring from a forty year business career. His interest includes history, motocycles, music and cooking.

Made in the USA
Columbia, SC
10 September 2022

66948835R00138